**Lee promised he wouldn't fight.
But how can he keep his word after this?**

Lee stopped short when he saw his locker. Half a dozen bright yellow feathers were taped to the front, along with a piece of notebook paper scrawled with the word "chicken." More yellow feathers were scattered on the floor.

Some of the kids in the crowd had picked up some of the feathers and were tickling each other with them. Then someone Lee couldn't see began to cluck like a chicken.

"Bawwwwkkkk! B-b-b-b-bawwwwkkkk!"

Everybody laughed. Lee wished he could disappear.

KARATE CLUB

Fight for Honor

CARIN GREENBERG BAKER

PUFFIN BOOKS

To Mom and Dad
with much love and thanks

PUFFIN BOOKS
Published by the Penguin Group
Viking Penguin, a division of Penguin Books USA Inc.,
375 Hudson Street, New York, New York 10014, U.S.A.
Penguin Books Ltd, 27 Wrights Lane, London W8 5TZ, England
Penguin Books Australia Ltd, Ringwood, Victoria, Australia
Penguin Books Canada Ltd, 10 Alcorn Avenue, Toronto, Ontario, Canada M4V 3B2
Penguin Books (N.Z.) Ltd, 182–190 Wairau Road, Auckland 10, New Zealand

Penguin Books Ltd, Registered Offices: Harmondsworth, Middlesex, England

First published in the United States of America by Puffin Books,
a division of Penguin Books USA Inc., 1992
1 3 5 7 9 10 8 6 4 2

Copyright © KidsBooks, Inc., 1992
All rights reserved

Library of Congress Catalog Card Number: 91-66631
ISBN: 0-14-036024-7

Printed in the United States of America
Set in Bookman

To win one hundred victories in one hundred battles is not the highest skill. To subdue the enemy without fighting is the highest skill.

—*Sun Tzu*

Chapter One

*It doesn't matter whom you're paired against;
your opponent is always yourself.*

—Nakamura

Lee Jenkins squatted low. He closed his eyes briefly to picture his imaginary opponent, also squatting, facing him. His imaginary opponent was just like Lee, exactly the same size, small and wiry, and ready to attack.

Lee imagined his opponent's solar plexus, the nerve center right below the rib cage. It was a key target. One good kick or punch there, and your opponent would double over, helpless and gasping.

Then Lee screamed as loud as he could. *"Ichi!"* he shouted, as his right fist shot forward and punched his imaginary opponent in the solar plexus. His left elbow flew back, pressing tight against his rib cage.

On either side of him, fourteen other right fists shot forward. Fourteen other left elbows tucked back.

"Ni!" Lee shouted. His left fist shot out, and his right elbow came back. Fourteen left fists and right elbows followed suit on either side.

"Go . . . roku . . . shichi . . . hachi . . . ku . . . ju!"

Lee was counting to ten in Japanese. On the tenth count, eleven boys and three girls, all dressed in white karate uniforms, all squatting like Lee, shouted together as loudly as they could.

"Hyah!"

This was called *kiai*—the focusing of energy and power in one sharp burst of sound. When Lee began his karate training, he'd been embarrassed to make such a loud sound. But that was five years ago, when he was only seven. Now he was twelve. Now he was a brown belt at the Midvale Karate Dojo. Kiai had become instinctive. So had the punches, kicks, and blocks he'd worked so hard to perfect. While Lee wasn't very big, he was a powerful fighter.

Lee had started karate after he'd moved to the United States from Vietnam. Lee's parents had died when he was a baby, and his grandfather had taken care of him after that.

Lee could still picture the old man's kind, wrinkled face. Lee also remembered their trips to the park when they lived in Vietnam. He would watch his grandfather practice Tai Chi, a Chinese form of self-defense, with dozens of other elderly people, their hands and feet sweeping in graceful circles.

Then, when Lee was six, his grandfather passed away. An American family, the Jenkinses, had adopted Lee. Now Lee had a new mother and father, and something he'd never had before, two brothers.

Though the Jenkins family had done its best to make Lee feel comfortable, Lee had been homesick when he first moved to Midvale. He didn't start to feel at home until the day they took him to the Midvale Mall. There, tucked between Plaza Shoes and Vinnie's Pizza, Lee had discovered the Midvale Karate Dojo. Just inside the *dojo*, or school, there was a long wall with windows that allowed Lee to look inside at the white-uniformed students practicing their moves in formation.

Lee had asked his new father if he could study there, and Stephen Jenkins had agreed. Soon both of Lee's brothers had also signed up for lessons. Michael Jenkins, one year older than Lee, and Jeremy, one year younger, proved as dedicated as Lee, and their training had brought them closer together. Lee and his brothers had even set up a mini-dojo in the basement of their house, complete with mirrors, weights, and a heavy bag hanging from the ceiling. Lee, Michael, and Jeremy practiced down there so often that their father nicknamed them "The Karate Club."

"Ichi!" shouted Michael Jenkins, squatting to Lee's right, as fourteen fists punched the air. His blond hair was damp with sweat, and his brown eyes were narrowed in concentration. Tall and athletic, Michael was one level behind Lee in his training. Michael had a green belt with brown tips.

As Michael continued the count, Lee searched for his other brother's reflection in the mirrored wall in front of him. Though Jeremy, too, was strong and had just earned his green belt, Lee always kept an eye on him. It wasn't because Jeremy was younger and smaller. It was because Jeremy always pushed himself too hard in class. Often he'd be so exhausted at the end of class that he barely had enough energy to bike home. He practiced so hard he wore himself out.

Sure enough, there was Jeremy, over on the far left. He was perspiring so heavily his uniform, or *gi,* looked like he'd taken a bath in it. Lee couldn't see the blue eyes behind Jeremy's round, wire-rimmed glasses, but he was sure they looked fierce. Sensei Davis was always telling Jeremy to relax, not to feel

4

anger. But Jeremy had trouble controlling himself. He was quick to anger, and karate was one way for him to let off angry steam without getting in trouble or hurting anyone.

People often teased Jeremy about having a hot temper to match his red hair. Lee knew it was just kidding, but it seemed true enough about Jeremy. Lee often marveled at how different his brothers were. Michael was calm and easygoing, a good problem solver. Jeremy was excitable and intense, the first one to lose his head in a difficult situation. Lee guessed he fell somewhere in between, neither as easygoing as Michael nor as quick-tempered as Jeremy. Together they made a good team.

"All rise," said Sensei Davis, motioning the class to get up from their squatting position. *Sensei* was Japanese for teacher, and Sensei Davis was the owner of the school. He was also a third degree black belt. A sturdily built man in his late thirties, Sensei Davis had straight, sandy hair and a sandy mustache to match.

Everyone stood up straight and shook out their tired legs. Squatting for long periods was really hard, especially on the upper thighs, but the more you did it, the stronger you got.

"Split the deck," said Sensei Davis, and the class

split into two lines on either side of the dojo. The training area was large and square with a polished wooden floor. At the front of the room were old black-and-white photographs of famous karate masters, hanging above the flags of Japan and the United States. The last photograph in the row was a picture of Sensei Davis, taken when he'd earned his black belt.

The back wall, near the dressing rooms, was the weapons wall. Hanging in neat rows along the wall were *bo,* long wooden staffs, *sai,* short metal swords, and *nunchuku,* two wooden rods connected by a short length of rope. Lee had started to learn the sai, now that he was a brown belt.

"Today we will work *jyu-kumite,* or freestyle fighting," Sensei Davis said. "Now, I realize you are all at different levels, so just use the techniques you know. Advanced pupils, I'm sure I don't have to remind you to go easy on the lower ranks. Do I have any volunteers?"

Lee moved toward the center of the floor, but his brothers had already beaten him there. They stood side by side, facing the sensei.

"Michael and Jeremy," the sensei said, "you're up."

Lee watched as his brothers slowly turned to face each other, waiting.

"*Kio-tsuke!*" The sensei called the boys to attention. They stood up very straight, hands at their sides.

"*Rei!*" The sensei gave the command to bow. Michael and Jeremy bowed, showing their respect for each other.

"*Onegai-shimasu,*" they said together. This meant "please teach me." Lee knew you said this before facing an opponent or demonstrating in front of an instructor. Instructors said it to their students too. The point was that anyone could learn from anyone else, even from a lower ranking student.

"*Yoi,*" the sensei called, and the boys held up their fists in the "ready" position.

"*Hajime!*" The sensei gave the command to begin, and Lee's brothers began to circle each other slowly. Suddenly, Jeremy's right foot flew out, aiming at Michael's solar plexus. Michael crossed his arms over his ribs, protecting his solar plexus, and at the last second, flung his left arm out at Jeremy's leg. Lee saw the arm connect, deflecting the kick. Michael followed it up with a right to the nose, pulling the punch just before it made contact. The point of jyu-kumite was not to actually injure your opponent in class, but to know you could if it were a real fight. If a blow did land, it could only land gently enough not to hurt.

7

As his brothers continued to circle around each other, Lee could see that Jeremy was wasting his energy. He aimed hard, rapid-fire kicks and punches. Sweat flew off his face as he struck and whirled. But his aim was off. He wasn't taking time to think about his offense, and his blows kept falling short. Michael, who was taller, had better reach and landed a lot more of his kicks and punches.

"Close the gap," the sensei directed Jeremy. "Make sure you hit the target."

"Arigato, Sensei!" Jeremy shouted at the top of his lungs.

Arigato was Japanese for thank you, the first word Lee had learned in karate. Lee had soon realized that you said thank you for everything, especially after receiving a correction from Sensei Davis. A lot of kids had a problem with this when they first started karate. Eventually, though, everybody realized that corrections made you stronger and better, and *that's* why you said thank you.

Jeremy moved in closer to Michael and landed a few punches. Then the sensei signaled them to stop. *"Yame!"* he called.

Lee's brothers immediately came to attention, bowed to each other, then turned and bowed to the sensei. "Arigato," they said, panting for breath.

"Two more volunteers," the sensei said.

This time, Lee was the first to arrive in the middle of the floor. Right behind him was Kevin Whittaker, a white belt. Kevin had only been at the dojo a few months, but he already acted like he knew everything about karate. Short and chunky, Kevin was in sixth grade with Lee and Jeremy. Lee had seen him in the lunchroom once or twice picking on some of the smaller kids, threatening to use his karate on them.

Lee had tried to speak to him about this once, telling Kevin this went against everything karate stood for. The first rule, the most important rule, was *Karate ni sente nashi*—there is no first attack in karate—but Kevin refused to listen. Kevin never listened to anybody. He thought that just because his older brother, Jason, was the biggest guy at Midvale Middle School and the best player on the football team, that he could pick on anybody he wanted. He was right, too. People let Kevin do whatever he wanted, even hit them, because they were even more afraid of what would happen if Jason got involved.

"Remember, Lee, he's a white belt, so no contact," the sensei said.

"Arigato, Sensei!" Lee said, bowing. Out of the corner of his eye, he could see Kevin screwing up his face in an angry grimace. Kevin probably thought he didn't need the protection the sensei was giving him.

Lee and Kevin bowed to each other and took their ready positions. When the sensei called *hajime*, Lee turned his body so only his left side was exposed. This helped keep two important targets, his solar plexus and his groin, out of Kevin's reach.

Kevin, on the other hand, faced Lee dead on, hopping from one foot to another, and throwing out punches like a shadow boxer. This was common with white belts. They didn't really know karate yet, so they tried to fight like guys in the movies or on TV. Kevin wasn't any different. His arms churned like windmills and he bounced up and down like a jumping bean. Lee didn't even have to block the punches because they never came close.

"More karate, Kevin," the sensei said. "Use your techniques." Lee wasn't surprised when Kevin neglected his "arigato" response, nor when the sensei overlooked it. The sensei was often more tolerant with new students. He knew it took a while to form good karate habits and manners.

Kevin reached further with his punches, but he aimed for Lee's chest and shoulders, and Lee easily deflected each blow. Kevin was already breathing hard and Lee hadn't done anything except block. Kevin aimed a kick at Lee's groin, but he took so long getting his leg out, Lee was gone before the kick landed. Lee could see Kevin was getting mad.

Then Kevin lost his temper. Completely forgetting his karate, he lunged forward, his fists flailing wildly. Lee took one smooth step to the side, grabbed the lapels of Kevin's gi, and swept one foot behind Kevin. Kevin flipped backward and would have hit the floor hard if Lee hadn't caught him at the last minute and lowered him gently by his lapels.

"Yame!" Sensei stopped them. "Good control, Lee."

Lee let go of Kevin's lapels. Kevin, red-faced, scowled up at him from the floor. After Kevin had risen to his feet, he barely bowed at Lee when the sensei gave the command, and he continued to scowl at Lee throughout the rest of the class.

"That was great, Lee," Jeremy congratulated him later in the locker room. "Your kumite is really strong."

The boys' locker room was long and narrow, with a row of gray metal lockers along the back wall. The opposite wall had a wooden bench with cubbyholes above and a curtained doorway leading out to the deck. There were also several showers and a small bathroom.

Lee, who was already showered and dressed, rolled

up his damp uniform and stuffed it in his blue canvas knapsack. "That was hardly a test of my kumite," he told his younger brother. "That wasn't even karate most of the time."

"Maybe not for him, but for you it was," Michael told him as he laced up his sneakers. "Your techniques were good, even if your opponent wasn't."

"Yeah, and you showed karate works in a street fight," Jeremy said, wiping his glasses clean with the bottom of his shirt. "The way Kevin was fighting was more like a real fight."

The curtain covering the doorway to the locker room was pushed aside, and Kevin Whittaker entered. His sullen green eyes glared at Lee from behind sweaty strands of curly brown hair. He slammed his locker open and began to get changed without bothering to shower.

Kevin continued to make as much noise as possible getting dressed, all the while maintaining a stony silence. Lee and his brothers looked at each other, uncertain about what to do. Jeremy looked like he was about to say something, then turned and headed for the door. Michael shrugged and stood up, shouldering his backpack.

Lee felt bad. It was obvious Kevin was upset about the kumite exercise. He just didn't understand karate,

Lee told himself. Maybe Lee could help him. The right thing for a more experienced student to do was to help someone less advanced.

Lee tried to break the tension. "Kevin, if you're interested, we could work on some techniques next time, before class."

"You've got to be kidding," Kevin said hotly. "After what you just did to me in class?"

"I didn't do anything," Lee said. "It was just an exercise."

"Yeah, right, tell me another," Kevin said. "You were just trying to make me look bad in front of the whole class."

"No way!" Jeremy said, defending his brother. "Lee would never do that."

"Who asked you, creep?" Kevin said nastily. "You think you're so hot. So what if you've been doing karate longer than me? Who cares? There's more than one way to fight."

"Come on, let's get out of here," Michael said. He headed toward the doorway, nudging Jeremy to head out with him.

Lee stood up to go, too, but Kevin stood in front of him. He stuck his chin in Lee's face. "Don't think this is over, punk, 'cause it's *not!* I'm gonna get even, and then you'll be sorry!"

13

Chapter Two

"Come off it, Kevin," Michael said over his shoulder. "Lee didn't do anything to you."

"*Didn't do anything?*" Kevin shouted in Lee's face. "You knocked me down! You used brown belt tricks to make me look bad. It wasn't a fair fight."

Lee just stared at Kevin in disbelief. Their sparring match was probably the biggest nonfight on record. Lee hadn't even blocked hard enough to give Kevin a bruise. He could have, of course, but he hadn't because Kevin was a white belt. White belts had to be treated gently. It was the rule.

"Nobody touches a Whittaker and gets away with it," Kevin said now. "Whittakers are winners! That's what my father always says. And no one better say any different."

There was no mistaking the look on Kevin's face.

Kevin was really furious. Lee felt he had to say something to calm him down.

"Uh . . . look, Kevin," Lee told him evenly, "this has nothing to do with winning or losing. We were just supposed to demonstrate some of the techniques we learned in class. I wasn't trying to beat you or make you look bad or anything like that. Let's just forget about it, okay?"

Lee tried to get past Kevin, but Kevin blocked his way again. "I don't forget stuff like that. Just you wait, jerkface."

Lee took a deep breath. Kevin was really beginning to make him angry, but he forced himself to stay calm.

"You can't get so upset every time a higher rank tags you in kumite," he said patiently. "It happens all the time. It's part of learning karate."

This time when Lee brushed past Kevin, he didn't try to stop him. But as the curtain swished closed behind him, Lee heard Kevin holler one last threat.

"Wait'll I tell my brother what you did," Kevin taunted. "He'll pulverize you so bad, you'll wish you'd never been born!"

Jeremy, who was waiting outside with Michael, rolled his eyes. "There he goes again, using his brother. Like that's the only way he could get even. He always says that, but it's just a bunch of hot air."

"I bet you're right," Michael said, as they stepped outside and headed toward the bike rack. "I know Jason, and he wouldn't beat anybody up. He's not a bully."

Lee couldn't have agreed more. Bullies were people with something to prove, but Jason Whittaker didn't have to prove anything to anybody. Jason was in eighth grade with Michael. He was also the most amazing football player who'd ever played for the Midvale Middle School Fighting Dragons. As quarterback of the team, he could throw with the accuracy and range of a guided missile. He was also the star linebacker, leading the team in tackles two years in a row. He was so good that the local newspaper and TV station sent reporters to cover the Dragons' weekly Friday football games.

They were just finished unlocking their bikes when Kevin burst out the front door of the dojo. Lee tried to ignore him as he got on his bike, but Kevin had no intention of letting him get away so easily.

"You better hurry home, chicken," he called. "Enjoy it while you can— before my brother destroys you."

Jeremy's eyes flashed and Lee could tell he was

dying to yell something back. "Let's go," Lee said, before his brother could open his mouth. He didn't want to make things any worse.

What he really felt like doing was throwing his bike on the ground, and giving Kevin an upper cut to the solar plexus. That would shut him up, all right. But he reminded himself that he was a brown belt, and Kevin was only a white belt. Kevin didn't know any better.

Besides, if Lee did hurt him, then he'd just be doing what Kevin was accusing him of. And he wasn't about to make Kevin's lies come true.

Most importantly, though, Lee couldn't fight Kevin even if he wanted to. *Karate ni sente nashi* was one of the most important rules. It meant Lee couldn't start a fight with anyone. He could only use his karate to defend if someone attacked him first.

As they rode out of the parking lot, Lee thought about what Kevin had said. He couldn't believe Kevin was so mad—or that he'd get his brother to beat him up. Even Michael agreed that Jason wouldn't do it. Still, Kevin had sounded so sure that Lee began to wonder. He didn't really know Jason Whittaker at all.

What if Jason Whittaker challenged Lee to a fight? He was much bigger and stronger than Lee. Lee wasn't sure his brown belt would be enough to save him. Then he remembered *karate ni sente nashi*. If Jason challenged him, Lee would just refuse to fight.

But he hoped it wouldn't get that far.

"What a jerk!" Jeremy said the next day, Tuesday, at lunch. The three brothers sat together in the Midvale Middle School cafeteria. Jeremy was talking about Kevin, of course, as he had been, nonstop, since yesterday afternoon.

Jeremy's plastic tray was loaded down with a cheeseburger, a double order of french fries, and two containers of chocolate milk. He sat across from Lee and next to Michael, at a brown Formica table that almost looked like real wood but wasn't. The large cafeteria was filled with rows and rows of tables just like this, filled with noisy sixth, seventh, and eighth graders.

"Kevin's always threatening people with his brother," Jeremy said indignantly. "I bet he's too scared to fight for himself." He took a big gulp of chocolate milk. Then he grabbed a handful of french fries and stuffed them in his mouth.

"I just hope he was bluffing," Michael said. "And that Jason doesn't get involved. He'd be hard to beat."

Lee, who sat on the hard Formica bench, picking at a tuna-fish sandwich, knew Michael was right. But getting beaten by Jason Whittaker wasn't what he was afraid of. He was afraid of how badly he'd wanted to smash Kevin.

After five years of studying karate, all it had taken was a few minutes for him to nearly forget everything he'd learned. He hadn't been able to empty his mind of anger, like Sensei Davis had taught them in class. He'd wanted to turn Kevin Whittaker into human shish kebab. If the sensei ever knew, he'd be disappointed in Lee. A true warrior never gave up his honor, and Lee had almost done that.

The only thing to do now was ignore Kevin Whittaker and pretend yesterday had never happened.

"Let's just stop talking about it, okay?" Lee told his brothers. "There's not going to be any fight."

"There should be, after what he said to you," Jeremy insisted, shoving more french fries into his mouth. "I wouldn't let him talk to me that way and get away with it."

"Chill out, Jeremy," Michael said. As usual, he was doodling, this time on his flattened lunch bag. Michael was a really good artist. Lee saw he was drawing a knight on horseback slaying a fantastic creature that was part dragon, part serpent, and part something else. Lee knew Michael hoped to work someday at Rocket Comics, where their mom was editor-in-chief.

"Kevin was just acting tough to save face," Michael went on. "I'm sure he's probably cooled down by now."

"I wouldn't be so sure," Jeremy said, glancing over Lee's shoulder.

Lee turned around, and felt a cold chill wash over him. Kevin Whittaker stood, halfway across the cafeteria, talking to a guy who was almost twice as tall as he was, and three times as wide. The guy wore a bright red football jersey with a big white number twelve on the front. Even if Lee hadn't watched the Fighting Dragons play every Friday, he would have had no trouble recognizing number twelve. No one else at Midvale Middle School took up so much room.

Kevin was talking to his brother, Jason Whittaker, and every few seconds he'd point toward Lee's table with an angry, stabbing motion of his finger. Jason turned to look at Lee, and his face showed annoyance.

"He doesn't look too happy," Jeremy said.

Kevin and Jason started walking across the lunchroom, heading right for Lee's table. They both had the same curly brown hair, chubby cheeks, and husky builds. They looked a lot like each other, except Kevin was the trial size, and Jason was the large economy size. Lee also noticed that Kevin was walking with a slight limp.

20

They stopped right in front of Lee, and Jason stared down at him. Lee had to tilt his head back just to meet Jason's eye. It was almost like Jason's head was perched on top of a huge mountain. And Lee was at the bottom.

"I hear you and my brother had a little problem yesterday," Jason said, his voice deadly calm.

Lee's heart was jumping around inside his chest like a pogo stick. He didn't like having Jason towering so far above him, so he stood up. He still didn't come up much past the big white number twelve on Jason's chest, but it was better than feeling like a midget.

Lee tried to push aside his fear the way the sensei had taught them. Lee imagined his mind as a lake. Right now the water was choppy with waves, but Lee focused on smoothing out the water until it was peaceful and still.

"There wasn't any problem," Lee said in an even voice. "We sparred in karate class. That's all."

"Kevin says you hurt him," Jason said. "He says you took advantage of him because he's a white belt.

"You kicked me right here," Kevin said, pointing to a spot on his leg. "Now it hurts me when I walk."

"That's not true!" Jeremy shouted, jumping up from the table. "My brother didn't do anything to him. It was a fair fight."

21

"Are you calling my brother a liar?" Jason asked, a sinister tone creeping into his voice. "That's like calling *me* a liar. The Whittakers stick together."

"Yeah!" Kevin said. He even stuck out his tongue.

Lee wanted to grab Kevin's tongue and yank it right out of his head. Talk about liars! Kevin must have made up a whopping story about their sparring match yesterday. And that fake limp was so obvious! Lee couldn't believe anyone would fall for that.

The worst part was, it was so unfair! Lee's actions had been completely correct yesterday in karate class. He'd done everything possible not to hurt Kevin. So why was Kevin going to so much trouble to pick a fight? Lee hoped Jason would be more willing to listen to reason than his little brother.

"What happened yesterday was just an exercise," Lee said, tilting his head back so he could meet Jason's eye. "Not a fight. I don't know what's wrong with Kevin's leg. He was walking fine at the dojo.

"So you *are* calling my brother a liar!" Jason exclaimed, moving forward so that all Lee could see was his broad chest and the number twelve. "Well, let me tell you this. Nobody picks on my family and gets away with it. You want to fight, then fight me!"

"You don't know who you're dealing with," Jeremy warned Jason. "Lee's a brown belt in karate."

Jason snickered. "I know you all think you're Bruce Lee with your fancy karate chops." He sliced his hands through the air and muttered some fake-Japanese words. "But I don't think your karate's going to help you much against *this*." He slid up the sleeve of his football jersey, exposing an arm that looked bigger than Lee's leg.

Lee stared at Jason's mass of muscles. He hated to admit it, but Jason had a point. Even though Lee's karate techniques were strong, they might not be effective against arms the size of Jason's. It might be like using karate against a tree.

On the other hand, just watching Jason make fun of karate, Lee knew he'd have the upper hand when it came to skill. It was clear from the way Jason moved that he didn't know much about fighting. If Jason had tried that in a fight, Lee could have easily avoided him and come back with some combination punches to the solar plexus and some kicks to the groin and ribs. Lee's arms and legs twitched just thinking about it.

But Lee's thoughts were running away with him again. The point was not how to fight, but how to avoid it. "I don't want to fight you," Lee said.

"That's 'cause you're scared," Kevin sneered.

"I'm not scared," Lee snapped back. "I'm just playing fair, and I wish you'd learn, too. Karate isn't about fighting. I'd be breaking the rules if I fought. I don't know why you don't get it."

"Don't talk to my brother that way," Jason said. "From now on, if you have anything to say, say it to me. And if I have something to say, I'll say it like this." Jason punched the palm of one hand with the other fist. "Anytime. Any place. I'm ready for you, Jenkins."

Still punching his palm, Jason lumbered away. Kevin remained behind.

"You don't fool me," he said with a laugh. "Karate has nothing to do with why you don't want to fight my brother. The real reason is you're chicken. *Bawk!*" he clucked. "Chicken!"

Jeremy practically climbed over the table in his eagerness to get at Kevin. "*You're* the one who's chicken!" he shouted. "You wouldn't be so brave if your big brother wasn't around!"

"You're just making it worse," Michael muttered. "Give it a rest, Jeremy, and butt out."

Kevin glared at Lee. "We'll see who's chicken," he said. Grabbing a handful of french fries off Jeremy's tray, Kevin turned and ran away.

"Hey!" Jeremy cried.

Despite his efforts to remain calm, Lee's heart was

thumping like a machine-gun when he sat down. "Relax and breathe," he said to himself, inhaling deeply. That's what the sensei always told them to do when they were tense. "Relax and breathe." But it was hard to relax after what had just happened. How had things gotten so out of control?

The more Lee thought about it, the angrier he became. Why should bullies have the right to do whatever they wanted, to bother people who were just minding their own business? It wasn't fair! Especially while he was forced, by his karate training, to do nothing about it. It made Lee want to smash something. Or someone.

"You're not going to fight Jason, are you, Lee?" Michael asked, his brown eyes worried.

"Not if I can help it," Lee said, poking holes in his tuna-fish sandwich with his finger. "But I was pretty tempted, just now, to use a couple of techniques on both of them."

"No kidding!" Jeremy exclaimed. "The guy's making trouble and he deserves to get it."

"That's no reason to fight him," Michael pointed out, picking up his pen again. Without even looking, he scribbled fangs and horns on the mythical beast on his lunch bag. "That's just as stupid as Jason fighting Lee because Lee beat his brother in kumite.

25

Besides, Jason's a lot bigger than Lee, and a lot heavier."

"But Jason doesn't have any training," Jeremy argued. "Lee's a lot quicker and I'm sure he's got better technique. I'll bet Lee knocks him out in two minutes flat. Boy, would I like to see that."

"Boy, would I like to see you drop it," Michael said.

Still poking at his sandwich, Lee listened miserably while his brothers argued. He'd never felt so confused in his entire life, and it was all because of karate!

Part of him wanted to bash Jason's face in, but, because of his karate training, Lee knew he couldn't do that. Lee had trained his arms and legs as effective weapons, but he'd also trained his mind. He remembered one of the quotes the sensei had put up on the bulletin board in the dojo, the one that said the greatest victory was not to win in battle but to subdue the enemy without fighting.

But that quote came from hundreds, maybe thousands of years ago when samurai wore kimonos and fought fierce, glorious battles, swords flashing in the forests. Could it really mean the same thing now, in this cafeteria with its buzzing fluorescent lights and tables sticky with grape juice and the smell of warm ketchup hanging in the air?

Rrrrrrrrring! The electronic bell went off, signaling the end of lunch period. Lee picked up his holey sandwich, and walked over to the trash can where he let it drop. He had hardly eaten anything, but it didn't matter. He wasn't hungry.

Ignoring the picture he'd drawn, Michael balled up his brown paper lunch bag and stood up. "I've got to go," he said, tossing the crumpled brown ball into the metal trash can several yards away. Then he patted Lee on the arm. "Don't let the Whittakers worry you," he said. "You did the right thing by refusing to fight. Sensei Davis would be proud of you."

Jeremy stuffed his last bite of cheeseburger in his mouth and picked up his lunch tray. "Mmmph!" he said.

Lee couldn't tell if that meant Jeremy disagreed, or if his mouth was just full of food. Lee wasn't even sure if *he* agreed. In the time he'd studied karate, he'd never had to put it to the test, to see if he really could control his anger and avoid a fight. And now he wasn't even sure he wanted to.

"Today," said Miss Wilson in her drawling voice, "we are going to learn about the microscope." Miss Wilson, Michael's science teacher, was a trim black woman in her midthirties. She stood behind the long counter that was her desk and work area, leaning on it with her elbows. The counter stretched nearly the whole width of the front of the room with two sinks in the middle. At one end of the counter stood about a dozen microscopes.

"Now," said Miss Wilson, "since we don't have enough microscopes for everyone, I'm going to team you up. When I call your names, come up to the front and take a microscope, then sit with your lab partner at any one of the double desks." Miss Wilson read from the list on her clipboard. "Addette Williams and Kathy Holohan. Jackie Bitterman and Bobby Di-Stanislao. Michael Jenkins and Suzanne Whittaker . . ."

Miss Wilson's voice droned on, but Michael didn't hear anything else. *Whittaker?* That name again! Michael had forgotten that Kevin and Jason had a sister—and she was in his science class! Michael had never spoken to her, so he didn't know if she was anything like Kevin. If she was, though, Michael didn't even want to talk to her, let alone be her lab partner.

With growing dread, Michael stood up and walked toward the counter. At the same time, a pretty girl with brown curly hair also walked to the front of the room. She was slender and tall, almost as tall as Michael.

"Any desk," said Miss Wilson, pointing to a microscope with her pen.

Michael reached for the microscope, but the girl beat him to it, cradling it in her arms. "I've got it," she said.

Michael followed her to a desk and sat down next to her.

"I'm Suzanne Whittaker," the girl said.

"Jason and Kevin's sister?" Michael asked, though he already knew the answer.

"Um . . . yeah. Jason and I are twins."

"Oh, great," Michael said glumly, staring at the scuffed black surface of the double desk. That was all he needed. Another Whittaker sitting right next to him. She looked like her brothers, too. She wasn't big and beefy like Jason, or small and beefy like Kevin, but she had the same curly brown hair and green eyes.

"And I already know a lot about microscopes if you have any questions," Suzanne added.

Michael already knew one thing. Suzanne was a show-off just like Kevin. And she'd probably try to take over in science class the same way Jason did on the football field.

"Science is my favorite subject," Suzanne said.

29

"How about you?"

Michael shrugged.

"What's the matter?" Suzanne asked. "Did I say something wrong?"

Michael focused his serious brown eyes on her. "You're a Whittaker," he said simply. "If we have to work together, fine, but we don't have to make small talk."

"What's that supposed to mean?" Suzanne asked, hurt.

"I'm a Jenkins," Michael said. "Your brothers are trying to pick a fight with my brother Lee. That puts us on opposite sides."

Suzanne sighed unhappily. "Not again," she said. "Kevin's always picking fights with people, and then he tries to rope Jason in, and I'm getting pretty tired of it. You know, half the school won't even talk to me just because I'm Kevin's sister? And the other half only talks to me because my twin is the star of the football team. Just once, I wish someone would look at me as *me*, and not someone's sister."

Now Michael looked at Suzanne a little more sympathetically. "I never really looked at it that way," he said. "I guess it isn't fair to lump you with your brothers. But I still don't like what's going on. I'd do anything to get Jason to forget about fighting Lee."

30

"So would I," Suzanne said. "And I'd like to put a muzzle on Kevin, while I'm at it."

Michael suddenly sat up straight. He had a great idea! "Look," he said, "neither of us wants our brothers to fight. Maybe we could work on this together, to stop them."

Suzanne looked interested. "It's worth a try," she said.

"Do you think you could talk to Jason? Michael asked. "Make him see there's really no reason to fight Lee." Michael explained what had happened in karate class between Lee and Kevin.

Suzanne nodded. "I see what you're saying. What happened in karate was just an exercise that Kevin volunteered for, so Jason's wrong in thinking he has to get revenge on Lee."

"Exactly," said Michael.

"I'll talk to him tonight," Suzanne promised.

Michael smiled for the first time since he'd met Suzanne. "Thanks a lot."

"All right," Miss Wilson said. "Everyone should have their microscopes in front of them by now, so let's begin."

31

Chapter Three

Wednesday, Lee coasted on his bike down the hill toward Midvale Middle School. It was a beautiful October morning. The sun was shining, the leaves were beginning to turn red and yellow and orange, and the wind whipped through his straight black hair. Lee felt so good, he could almost forget about what had happened yesterday in the lunchroom.

Jason Whittaker had passed him twice in the halls in the afternoon and hadn't even looked at him. Then Lee had seen Kevin at the dojo after school, and Kevin hadn't said a word. Maybe the Whittakers had forgotten about the fight. Maybe they'd realized it wasn't worth it.

As Lee neared the school, Jeremy, also on his bike, swerved in front of him, pedaling furiously. Michael was already at school because he had an early meeting of the school newspaper, the *Monitor*. Michael was the layout artist and also drew an occasional cartoon.

His legs still churning, Jeremy turned right into the driveway. He sped past the lawn leading up to the football field, braked sharply at the bike rack, and hopped off.

"Beat you!" said Jeremy, grinning, as Lee pulled up beside him. Jeremy was sweating and his chest was heaving up and down.

"I didn't know it was a race," Lee said, coming to a gentle stop and stepping off his bike.

"It's *always* a race," Jeremy said. "That's what makes it fun."

"It's fun just riding," Lee said. He threaded his chain through the spokes of his front wheel and locked it to the metal rack. "Sensei Davis says we shouldn't be so competitive. If we focus too hard on where we're going, we can miss out on a lot along the way."

"That's in karate," Jeremy said. "This is bike riding and that's completely different."

Jeremy locked his bicycle and the two brothers headed for the back entrance to the sixth-grade wing. Though Lee was a year older than Jeremy, they were in the same grade. Lee hadn't come to the United States until he was six years old and he hadn't spoken any English, so his parents had started him in kindergarten instead of first grade.

"Kevin sure was quiet yesterday at the dojo," Jeremy said. "I guess we won't be hearing from the Whittakers again. I always knew Kevin was full of hot air."

"That's what I was thinking," Lee said as Jeremy held open the back door. They entered a long hallway with a beige linoleum floor. On either side of the hall were rows of beige metal lockers, broken up by classroom doors. Already the hall was filled with kids.

As Lee passed a group of girls from his math class, he thought he saw them giggle and whisper and look at him. Lee felt a chill go down his spine. Was his hair sticking up again? It did that sometimes, just a few strands, sticking straight up in the air no matter how much he brushed them down. Nervously, Lee touched the top of his head. His hair lay flat, the way it was supposed to.

Then a more horrible thought hit him. He quickly looked down. His zipper was okay, too. He must have been imagining things.

There was a big crowd of kids near Lee's locker, more than the usual morning rush crowd.

"Excuse me," Lee said, as he and Jeremy tried to push their way through.

A slight boy with straight blond hair turned when

he saw Lee. Then he whispered something to the boy next to him and stepped aside, still looking at Lee.

Lee stopped short when he saw his locker. Half a dozen bright yellow feathers were taped to the front, along with a piece of notebook paper scrawled with the word "chicken." More yellow feathers were scattered on the floor.

Lee felt his face grow hot with embarrassment. There was no question who had left that message. The Whittakers hadn't forgotten after all.

Some of the kids in the crowd had picked up the yellow feathers and were tickling each other with them. When they saw Lee, though, they stopped and stared. Some snickered and pointed. Then someone Lee couldn't see began to cluck like a chicken.

"Bawwwkkkk! B-b-b-b-bawwwwkkkk!"

Everybody burst out laughing. Lee wanted to turn and run back down the hall. He wanted to bicycle home as fast as he could and hide under the covers. But he couldn't. If he ran away, then he'd really look like a chicken. Lee tried to imagine the lake inside his mind again, with its choppy water. He tried to calm down, to smooth the water. But he was too nervous to think of anything except how stupid he felt.

Jeremy wasn't nervous, though. He was furious, his face redder than his hair. "Shut up!" he screamed at the crowd. "Get away from my brother's locker or else!"

"Or else what?" asked the boy with the blond hair. "Your brother will lay a rotten egg?"

Everybody laughed. Lee wished he could disappear.

"For your information," Jeremy yelled, "my brother is a brown belt in karate. He can break boards with his bare hand. He could break your head like that!" He snapped his fingers.

Everyone stepped back when they heard this. Several of the kids began to drift down the hall. Soon things were back to normal. Sort of. The few kids who remained had turned away and were whispering among themselves.

"Jeremy...," Lee hissed at his brother. "You're not supposed to say stuff like that about karate. That's not what it's for ... "

"It's true, isn't it?" Jeremy argued. "And look. It worked."

"Breaking boards is only a small part of karate," Lee said. "Sensei Davis would get really angry if he heard you talk like that."

"Well *I'm* really angry," Jeremy said. "And you should be too. You can't let them get away with this."

"I'm not gonna let them think they got to me," Lee

said. "That'd just be giving them what they want."

"You're not going to just take it, are you?" Jeremy exclaimed.

"No," Lee answered. "But I'm not going to let it bother me, either."

"How are you going to do that?" Jeremy demanded.

"I'm going to empty my mind of all thoughts," Lee said, quoting what the sensei told them at the beginning of each karate class. At the beginning of class, the students lined up in two rows, front to back, facing the sensei. At the sensei's command, everyone bowed and sat down on the floor in *seiza* position, legs folded underneath them, hands crossed in their laps. Then the sensei told them to empty their minds, to push negative thoughts out of their heads until they were feeling peaceful and quiet inside.

Lee had always found this one of the hardest exercises. No matter how hard he tried to think of nothing, yammering voices in his skull would wonder what was for dinner, or remind him of a homework assignment, or worry about how he did on a test. Today in the hallway it was even harder because all the voices were yelling together *"Punch their lights out!"*

But Lee had to silence the voices. He had to use mental discipline to gain control. If he couldn't do it in this situation, then what had he studied karate for?

37

Maybe Lee wasn't an ancient samurai warrior, and maybe he carried a knapsack instead of a sword, but the Whittakers were real enemies, no doubt about it.

"I can't let them control my thoughts," Lee said. "The important thing is to stay calm."

"This is no time to stay calm!" Jeremy exclaimed. "This is war!" He slammed his hand against Lee's locker and several fluffy yellow feathers came unstuck and floated gently to the floor.

Lee knelt down and scooped up the feathers. Then he ripped off the "chicken" note and the remaining feathers and shoved them all into the side pocket of his knapsack. "It's over," he told his brother, standing up.

Jeremy looked at Lee intently through his wire-rimmed glasses. "Mental discipline's not the only thing we learn in karate," Jeremy said. "Karate's trained us to fight back, not to just stand there. Kevin's the one who started it. You'd just be defending yourself if you bashed him."

"Cluck! Cluck! Cluck!" came a high-pitched voice from down the hall.

Lee and Jeremy turned around but they couldn't see through all the people milling around the hallway.

"CLUCK! CLUCK! CLUCK!" The voice was

38

louder this time. Even before Lee spotted the short, chunky body and curly hair, he knew who it was.

"CHICKEN!" Kevin Whittaker screamed at Lee, flapping his thick arms like they were wings. Everybody laughed. Kevin, enjoying the attention, started strutting in a circle like a bird, his head jerking forward and back, his arms still flapping.

"Chicken!" several people chimed in.

Kevin stopped flapping and faced Lee. "You ready to face my brother now, Jenkins?" he sneered.

Though Lee's legs felt rubbery and his stomach had tied itself in knots, Lee turned his back on Kevin. With shaking hands, he started working the combination on his locker. It wasn't that he was scared of Kevin, or even Jason. He just felt incredibly embarrassed that everyone was watching.

"You deaf, Jenkins?" Kevin shouted in Lee's ear. "I'm talking to you!"

Lee dialed the last number on his lock and pulled the door open. Several more yellow feathers wafted out of the locker, one landing in his hair. Lee brushed it off and began unloading the books from his knapsack and piling them in the bottom of his locker.

"I know what your act is," Kevin said. "You think you're going to psych me out with your stupid 'Ninja' attitude. But I'm not gonna quit till you give in. You'll fight my brother, and when you do he's gonna turn you into hamburger."

"You won't get away with this!" Jeremy shouted.

Kevin smiled meanly. "You want to fight, too? I'm sure my brother will take you on," he said. "Both of you at the same time, even. You'd be like fleas to him. He could squash you with one finger."

"I'll squash you," Jeremy said taking a fighting stance, clenched fists blocking his face and chest, his body turned to the side.

"No, you won't," Lee said, stepping between them. "This has nothing to do with you."

"Let me at 'im," Jeremy said through gritted teeth. "If his brother will fight for him, then I'll fight for you."

"That's so touching," said Kevin, pretending to wipe a tear from his eye. "But I know you're really a chicken, Jeremy, just like your brother. I guess that makes your house a chicken coop, doesn't it!" Kevin laughed at his own joke. So did several boys and girls standing nearby.

Rrrrrrrrrrring! First period was about to begin.

"Saved by the bell," said Kevin. "This time. Next time you won't be so lucky."

Still clucking and squawking, he strutted down the hall.

Michael paced up and down the center aisle of the cafeteria, anxiously searching the tables for his brothers.

Lee and Jeremy weren't sitting down, and they weren't waiting on line at the hot lunch counter or the snack bar. Where were they? They couldn't be in the nurse's office, could they? Had something happened?

Then Michael noticed Suzanne Whittaker, sitting by herself, eating a sandwich.

Michael walked up to her table. "Is it okay if I sit here?" he asked.

Suzanne looked up and smiled. "There's plenty of room," she said. Then she saw Michael's worried expression. "I guess you heard," she said grimly.

Michael tossed his brown paper bag on the table, climbed over the bench, and sat down. Then he unscrewed the cap from his bottle of grape juice and chucked the cap at the trash can across the aisle.

"Heard what?" Michael said carefully. He had a bad feeling about this.

Suzanne put down her sandwich. "Kevin stuck

41

feathers all over Lee's locker and called him a chicken. I didn't know he was going to do it, I swear, or I'd have tried to stop him."

"Did you have a chance to talk to your brothers last night?" Michael asked.

"I tried," Suzanne said, her green eyes anxious. "I told Kevin why he shouldn't have gotten so upset about what happened in karate class, but he wouldn't listen to me. He said he knows more about karate than I do, so I should mind my own business."

Michael emptied out his lunch bag, which contained a peanut butter and jelly sandwich, an apple, and a small bag of potato chips. Then he smoothed out the brown paper bag and took a pen out of his pocket. "What about Jason?" he asked, starting to sketch the outline of a chicken.

"I couldn't get near him long enough to say anything," Suzanne answered. "He had football practice after school, then he was raking leaves for about ten different people in the neighborhood so he didn't get home until after dark, then he did his homework and went to sleep."

"What about dinnertime?" Michael asked. "Could you talk to him then? That's when my family talks about stuff."

Suzanne picked up a cellophane-wrapped package of cookies and became very interested in reading the ingredient list. After a minute, she looked up at Michael and her eyes had an unreadable expression. "We're all on different schedules in my family," she said. "Dinner's a more . . . casual thing. You know. Besides, I don't want to bring it up around my parents."

Michael sort of understood. Usually, his dad prepared dinner because he got home first and liked to cook. Then everyone else would pitch in when they got home. But sometimes his mother worked late or his father had to go out of town on business. Whichever parent was left would usually take the boys out for pizza.

"Thanks for trying," Michael said. He looked down at the chicken he'd drawn on his lunch bag. He was startled to see that its face looked a lot like Kevin Whittaker's. He hadn't even realized he'd done that. He hastily crumpled up the bag before Suzanne could see it.

"I wish I could think of something else we could do," Suzanne sighed. "We're smart people. There's got to be a way."

Michael took a long swig of grape juice, then looked

around again for his brothers. He spotted Jeremy's red hair as his youngest brother carried a heavily loaded tray from the lunch line. Lee was right behind him, carrying a brown paper bag.

"Over here!" Michael waved.

Lee spotted Michael first and tapped Jeremy on the shoulder. A few seconds later, they were sitting down with Michael and Suzanne.

Jeremy looked from Michael to Suzanne and back to Michael again. Michael knew what that look meant. It meant "What are you doing sitting with a *girl*?" Michael didn't mind girls as much as he used to, but Jeremy thought they were useless.

Michael knew Jeremy would understand, though, when he introduced Suzanne. "This is Suzanne *Whittaker*," he said, emphasizing the last name.

Jeremy's blue eyes grew large and round, magnified by his thick glasses. "Jason's sister?" he asked, shocked. "You're sitting with *Jason's sister?*"

"We're trying to stop the fight," Michael said. "She's been talking to Kevin . . . "

"I'll *bet* she's been talking to Kevin," Jeremy said angrily. "She's probably his spy and reporting every word you say to him!"

"That's not true!" Suzanne said angrily.

44

"How can you trust her?" Jeremy said, ignoring Suzanne. "She's a Whittaker!"

"That's what I thought at first, too," Michael said. "But wait . . . "

"Come on, Lee," Jeremy said, rising from the bench and picking up his tray. "We're not eating lunch with anyone named Whittaker."

Lee remained seated, looking uncertainly from Jeremy to Michael.

"Are you coming?" Jeremy asked impatiently.

"Don't bother!" Suzanne exclaimed, stuffing the rest of her lunch into a brown paper bag and standing up. "You can have the stupid table. I certainly wouldn't want to share it with anyone named *Jenkins!*"

Suzanne climbed over the bench and stalked off. Lee thought her eyes looked very bright—as if there were tears in them.

"Thanks a lot, Jeremy," Michael said. "She was trying to help us, and now you insulted her. That was really rude, you know that?"

"I don't have to be nice to her," Jeremy protested. "She's just like her brothers."

"You don't know her," Michael argued. "She's *not* like them—she's really nice."

45

Jeremy's eyes blinked rapidly behind his glasses. "I can't believe you're defending her!" he yelled, pounding on the table with his fist. "Don't you stick up for your own brothers anymore? *Whose side are you on?*"

Chapter Four

Lee felt awful. It was bad enough Jason wanted to fight him, but now his brothers were fighting with each other! "Stop it!" he said to Michael and Jeremy. "This has nothing to do with you. This is between the Whittakers and me, not you."

"You're totally wrong," Jeremy said. "This is a family matter. The whole thing started because of you and Kevin. Now Jason's threatening you, and Kevin started with me. It's us against them! If Michael weren't such a . . . a *traitor,* he wouldn't even talk to *her!*"

Michael's jaw tensed. "I'm trying to tell you Suzanne isn't like her brothers."

"Maybe you just don't know her yet," Jeremy said.

"Oh, and you do?" Michael challenged him.

"Of course not!" Jeremy exclaimed. "I'm not friends

with any *girl!* Anyway, I'm right, you know I am."

"You are not," Michael said angrily.

So where does that leave me? Lee wanted to say.

As Jeremy turned away from Michael and Michael turned away from Jeremy, Lee knew the answer to his question. He was left with two brothers who weren't speaking to each other. And somehow he felt it was all his fault.

"So, we goin' to the game on Friday?" Lee asked Jeremy after school that day. The Fighting Dragons were playing their archrivals the Weston Warriors at home. Michael was with them. It was after school and they were walking toward the bicycle rack.

Every Friday during the fall, the middle school's football team played one of the other middle schools in the area. The Jenkins brothers hadn't missed a game yet. Lee knew he wasn't going to enjoy the game as much as usual because of his problem with the Whittakers, but he was determined not to let it affect what he did. He wasn't going to stop going to games just because Jason was the star of the team.

"I don't know if I'm going," Jeremy said, scowling.

"Why not? We always go."

Jeremy glared at Michael out of the corner of his eye. "I'm not going if *he* goes."

Michael said nothing.

"Oh, come on, you guys!" Lee said. "Quit fighting. Especially over this, okay? It's my problem, not yours."

Michael just pressed his lips together in a thin line.

Lee arrived at the bike rack first and leaned down, reaching for the chain threaded around his front wheel. But before he'd even touched it, he realized something horrible had happened. There wasn't any point in unlocking his bike, because he wasn't going to be able to ride it.

Lee's front tire had been slashed and several yellow feathers were sprinkled on the pavement. Kevin had struck again, and this time it was worse than embarrassing. It was criminal.

"What's the matter?" Jeremy asked, seeing the shocked expression on Lee's face.

Lee simply pointed to his front tire. Michael and Jeremy ran forward at the same time to examine it.

"I can't believe they did that!" Michael exclaimed. "That's really dirty!"

"He's scum!" Jeremy agreed, his fight with Michael temporarily forgotten. He clenched his fists and uttered a loud *kiai*. "*Hyaaaaaah!*" he screamed, screwing up his face. "If Kevin were here right now, I'd break his arms with some serious karate chops!"

Lee felt exactly the same way. He tried again to calm down, but it was impossible. His heart was beating too wildly and the blood was roaring through his veins. He looked up the grassy hill toward the nearby football field to see if Kevin was watching Jason practice, as he usually did, but no one was there yet. Lee was relieved. If he'd seen Kevin at this moment, he might have lost control completely, Jason or no Jason.

"I really feel like breaking Kevin's ribs," Lee muttered. "Or any other bone that gets in my way."

"That's the spirit!" Jeremy cheered. "Smash his face, break his nose! Show your stuff, Lee."

"Don't," Michael said. "He hurt your property, not your body. You can't attack him for this."

"There you go siding with the Whittakers again!" Jeremy yelled, his anger at Michael returning. "Why don't you just move in with them, you like them so much!"

Michael looked at Jeremy coldly. "Is there a fly around here? I keep hearing this annoying buzz."

"I'll buzz *you!*" Jeremy threatened. Michael ignored him.

"Come on, Lee," Michael said. "I'll walk my bike with you to the dojo. But we'd better walk fast, or we'll be late for karate class."

"No, *I'll* walk my bike with you," Jeremy said. "Two's company, three's a crowd."

"Let's all go together," Lee said tensely.

In uncomfortable silence, the three brothers wheeled their bicycles down the hill, toward the Midvale Mall. Within a few minutes, they'd reached the side road that led to the mall's vast parking lot. There was room for at least a thousand cars, but the lot was less than half full.

Lee, Michael, and Jeremy cut through the parking lot to the wide sidewalk running alongside the row of stores, restaurants, and a twelve-plex movie theater. They passed Plaza Shoes. Next was the plate glass window with the words *Midvale Karate Dojo* neatly lettered in red ink. Beneath the words was a red satin banner with a gold circle embroidered on it. Inside the circle was a clenched fist over crossed *sai*, slender pointed weapons that looked like short swords. The brothers locked their bikes on the nearby rack and pushed open the glass door.

The entrance to the Midvale Karate Dojo was plate glass. Just inside was another wall with windows starting halfway up so people outside could see into the classroom. Beneath the windows, all along the wall, were framed photographs of children and adults in gi, posing in groups or demonstrating techniques.

Toward the right of the interior wall was the curtained doorway to the classroom.

On the left, halfway along the wall was another door. This led to the sensei's private office. On the right wall, there was a curtained closet. Lee, Michael and Jeremy stopped by the closet and removed their shoes, placing them on the wooden shelves inside. Shoes weren't allowed in the classroom.

Michael pulled the curtain aside, leading to the training area. The brothers bowed to the photographs of the ancient masters, showing their respect for their teachers. Then they padded in their socks across the wooden deck toward the boys' locker room and bowed again before leaving the classroom.

In the locker room, a few boys were already changing into their gi. One of them was Kevin Whittaker. He sneered when he saw Lee.

"Have a nice ride?" he sneered.

"How could I?" Lee said, gritting his teeth. "You slashed my front tire."

"I told you you'd be sorry for what you did to me," Kevin said, tightening the waist strings of his white cotton gi pants and tying a double knot.

"I didn't do anything to you," Lee said, trying not to yell. "If you're going to start crying every time a higher rank beats you in kumite, you shouldn't study karate."

"You were trying to make me look bad," Kevin insisted stubbornly. "But my brother will make you look even worse. *Chicken! Bawwwkkkk!*"

Lee was clenching his jaw so hard he was beginning to get a headache.

"I'll bet you'd like to punch me right now, wouldn't you?" Kevin goaded Lee.

"I'd like to do a lot more than that," Lee said.

"But you can't," Kevin mocked him. "Not in karate class. I'm only a white belt. The sensei would get mad if you tried anything. Not to mention my brother . . . "

The pressure in Lee's head was growing so bad he thought he would explode. He wanted to punch the wall, the locker, anything. Mostly, he wanted to punch Kevin. Still grinning, Kevin shoved past Lee out of the locker room.

"Come on, Lee," Michael said quietly. "Let's get dressed."

The Jenkins brothers changed into their gi and tied on their colored belts. Then they pushed aside the curtain, bowed toward the flags, and ran out to the deck. A few seconds later, Sensei Davis entered the deck from his office. Everyone immediately stopped what they were doing, turned to him, and bowed.

"*Onegai-shimasu, Sensei!*" they shouted together. Please teach me. The sensei bowed, too. "*Onegai-shimasu,*" he said in his soft, hoarse voice. "*Shugo,* line up!"

The students ran toward the wall with the flags and formed two lines leading straight back. They were arranged in rank order, with brown belts first, then green belts with brown tips, then green belts, down to white belts in the back. There were no black belts because this was a class for kids. A person had to be at least eighteen years old to get a black belt.

The sensei stood beneath the flags, facing them. Lee, the highest ranking student, stood at the front of the line on the left.

"Sit, *seiza,*" the sensei said.

Everyone folded their legs underneath them, crossed their hands in their laps, and closed their eyes.

"Now empty your mind of all thoughts," the sensei instructed them. "If a thought comes into your head, push it out again."

Lee tried his best to do as the sensei said, but he kept seeing Kevin's face in his mind, laughing and jeering. No matter how many times he pushed the face away, it kept coming back. Instead of calming down, Lee was feeling more angry and frustrated.

The sensei clapped his hands. Everyone opened their eyes. The class bowed again to the pictures of the ancient masters, then jumped to their feet to begin their warm-up. They stretched their necks, arms, and legs. They jumped up and down. Then Sensei told the two lines to face each other.

"Today," the sensei said, "we'll start with arm training. I know some of you are new, so I'll explain. Since we use our arms as weapons, we have to toughen them up so you won't be afraid of making contact. Lee, Alyse, please demonstrate."

Lee stood at attention and bowed to the brown belt facing him, Alyse Walker, a tall, slim girl whose straight black hair was pulled back in a ponytail. Alyse bowed back. They squatted and swung their right arms down toward each other, banging them together. Alyse's bony arm felt like a knife slicing into his arm, but Lee didn't mind the pain. He was used to it. Then they lifted their right arms up and banged them again, then dropped them and banged them one more time. They twisted their hips and repeated the same thing with their left arms, then started again on the right, going faster and faster. Down, up, down! Down, up,

55

down! Bang, bang, bang! Bang, bang, bang!

Lee had always had good self-control with arm training, but now he felt himself getting carried away. Maybe it was because of the image of Kevin's face that still hung in his mind. As the pace picked up, Lee found himself hitting harder and harder. Alyse kept up with him, her arms banging his in rhythm, but she looked at him once as if to say *What are you doing?* Lee knew they were hitting too hard, but he couldn't stop himself.

"*Yame!* Stop!" the sensei said.

Lee and Alyse broke apart and bowed to each other. "Arigato!" they said, thanking each other.

"That was too much, Lee," the sensei said. "I don't want anybody to do it full speed, full power. Just do it three-quarter speed and emphasize turning your hips as you change arms."

"Arigato, Sensei!" Lee shouted. He was already dripping with sweat.

"Step down and change opponents!" the sensei called, and the two lines moved in opposite directions. "Now everyone will do the exercise."

"*Hajime!*" The sensei commanded them to begin.

Lee faced his next opponent, Dwight Vernon, a green belt with brown tips. They bowed, then squatted, and began to bang arms. Again, Lee found himself hitting harder than he meant to. It was like an unseen force was pushing him, making him slam his arms against Dwight's with all his might. He could tell Dwight didn't want to hit that hard, but he couldn't stop himself.

"*Yame!*" came the sensei's voice right behind Lee. The two lines broke apart. "Lee," the sensei said, "I just finished telling you not to go full speed and power. Since you can't follow directions, give me twenty-five push-ups. Everyone else, switch places."

As the lines moved past each other again, Lee dropped down to the floor and began doing push-ups, counting in Japanese. "Ichi, ni, san, shi, go, roku . . . " He knew he'd really screwed up, and it was all because of Kevin and Jason. If they hadn't made him so mad, he never would have lost control in class. Now Sensei Davis was mad at him too. Things just kept getting worse and worse.

By the time he got to his twenty-fourth push-up, Lee thought his arms were going to break. But he couldn't stop now. He wouldn't give Kevin the satisfaction. He knew Kevin was probably secretly laughing at him already. Lee finished the last one and hopped to his feet. The sensei motioned him to rejoin the line.

At the end of class, everybody lined up the way

they had at the beginning, sat on the floor, and closed their eyes. This time Lee had less trouble emptying his mind, mostly because he was too exhausted to think about anything. The Whittakers were wearing him out! The sensei clapped his hands and everyone jumped to their feet.

"Arigato, Sensei!" they shouted.

"Arigato," the sensei said. Lee started to turn toward the locker room, but the sensei motioned for him to stay. "I'd like to talk to you in my office," he said.

Uh oh, Lee thought. Now he was really in trouble.

Lee stood aside while Sensei Davis bowed to the flags and entered his office. Then Lee bowed and followed the sensei inside. The sensei's office was small with a battered brown desk with an old cushioned chair on wheels behind it and a few wooden chairs. The wall behind the desk was covered with more photographs of students and three framed certificates with Japanese writing on them. The certificates showed when Sensei Davis had been promoted to first, second, and third degree black belt.

The sensei sat down behind his desk and pointed to a wooden chair. Lee sat down.

"Is something wrong, Lee?" Sensei asked kindly.

His brown eyes were so dark they didn't seem to have any pupils.

Lee had expected something much worse. He'd thought the sensei would yell at him. But even though the sensei was being nice, Lee didn't know how to answer. His problem with Kevin and Jason didn't really have that much to do with karate, even though that's where the whole thing had started.

Lee shook his head. "No, Sensei," he said.

"Are you sure?" the sensei asked. "Are you having problems at home or at school?"

Lee sighed. Part of him wanted to open up to the sensei, ask his advice how to handle the Whittakers. But an even bigger part was ashamed—ashamed that he'd lost control, ashamed that he couldn't solve the problem himself. He was a brown belt! He should feel more sure of himself by now. He should know how to solve his own problems.

"There is a problem, Sensei," Lee finally admitted. "But I'd really like to find my own solution."

The sensei nodded and scratched his sandy-colored mustache. "Fine," he said, "but make sure you don't take it out on the other students."

"Yes, Sensei," Lee said.

The sensei stood up and Lee started to leave.

"Lee . . . " Sensei said, stopping him.

Lee turned back to Sensei Davis.

"If you *don't* find the solution, you can always come back and talk to me."

"Arigato, Sensei!" Lee said and bowed.

"Arigato!" the sensei said.

Chapter Five

The walk home from the dojo had never seemed so long to Lee. It was bad enough his tire was slashed, but Michael and Jeremy didn't say a word to each other the whole time. Lee didn't feel much like speaking, either. He was still too embarrassed about getting called in to the sensei's office.

When they finally reached their house, Lee, Michael, and Jeremy parked their bikes in the garage and opened the door leading into the kitchen. Their father was already at the stove, tossing onions into a frying pan.

"Hi, guys," Stephen Jenkins called to his sons. He was tall and well-built, with straight blond hair the same shade as Michael's and wire-rimmed glasses like Jeremy's. He was in his late thirties, but he looked younger, mostly because of the way he dressed. Today, he was wearing faded, sloppy jeans and a tee-shirt that said "Save Our Planet."

A former army officer, Mr. Jenkins was now director of the county recycling center. Since he got off work earlier than Mrs. Jenkins and since he liked to cook, he made dinner every weeknight. Lee and his brothers helped, too. In fact, the boys' nightly assignments were posted on a duty roster stuck to the refrigerator.

"You ready to take your stations?" Lee's father asked, as he did every night.

Usually, Lee, Michael, and Jeremy saluted crisply and said "Yes, sir!" But today they just walked silently to the refrigerator and checked their assignments. Lee was on salad. Jeremy had to set the table, and Michael's job was to mash the potatoes.

"How was your day?" Mr. Jenkins asked as they all got to work.

Lee just stuck his head inside the refrigerator and muttered under his breath.

"What was that?" Mr. Jenkins asked.

Lee poked his head above the door and said glumly, "Not so great."

Mr. Jenkins looked concerned. "What's wrong?" he asked.

Lee pulled lettuce out of the refrigerator and a glass salad bowl out of the cabinet. Then he began shredding the lettuce into tiny pieces, pretending the lettuce was Jason and Kevin Whittaker. "It's nothing you can help me with," he told his father.

Just then, they heard the electronic garage door open.

"Mom's home!" said Mr. Jenkins.

They heard the purring sound of an engine as the car pulled into the garage. Everybody stopped what they were doing and turned expectantly as the door from the garage opened.

"Helloooo!" came Andrea Jenkins's musical voice. She was hidden behind two bulging brown grocery bags she was carrying.

"Andrea, where are you?" Mr. Jenkins asked, pretending to be alarmed. "Where's my wife? What have you done with my wife?"

Lee's mother put the bag down on the kitchen table and smiled at her family. She was petite but strong, with coppery red hair, and a sprinkling of freckles across her nose. Her eyes were clear blue, and the bright blue dress she wore made them look even bluer.

"How are all my men?" she asked as her sons and husband came over to kiss her.

"*I'm* fine," Mr. Jenkins said, "but I don't know about the rest of these guys."

"Is there a problem?" Mrs. Jenkins asked.

Lee didn't answer. He felt bad keeping something from his parents, but things had gotten complicated enough without getting them involved, too. Lee knew the first thing his dad would do when he heard about the slashed tire would be call Mr. Cefari, the vice principal. Then Mr. Cefari would call Mr. and Mrs. Whittaker. Then Kevin and Jason would know Lee was a tattletale and a crybaby. It was bad enough they thought he was chicken.

"Maybe if we feed them, they'll talk," Mrs. Jenkins said, carrying her bags to the counter and putting the groceries away.

A few minutes later, when they were sitting around the table, Mr. Jenkins turned to Lee. "So what happened today?" he asked. "Was there trouble at school?"

Lee sighed. "Yes," he said, "but it's a long story."

"I love stories," Mrs. Jenkins said, propping up one elbow on the dinner table and resting her head on the palm of her hand. "And I've got all the time in the world."

Lee avoided his mother's piercing eyes. "I'd really

rather figure this out myself," he said.

"Can't you at least give us a hint?" his mother pleaded. "The suspense is killing me!"

As bad as Lee felt right now, he had to laugh. Sometimes his mother acted like a little kid. "It's just some guys at school," Lee said. "But don't worry. I can handle it."

"When you do," Mr. Jenkins said, "make sure you handle it with your head, not your fists. Fighting won't solve anything. I know from my own experience."

Mr. Jenkins pulled up the sleeve of his tee-shirt to show a jagged scar across his shoulder. "You've seen my souvenir from Vietnam," he said, "from the grenade that nearly blew my arm off. And for what? There was no point to that war, or any wars. If people put the same amount of energy into solving their problems peacefully as they do fighting, the world would be a much better place."

Lee plunked both elbows on the table and rested his chin in his hands. Was his father a mind reader? It was almost as if his father knew what was going on without being told. But even though Lee knew his father was right, he also knew it wasn't as simple as his father made it sound. You couldn't discuss things peacefully with people like Kevin and Jason.

But something his father said gave Lee an idea. His father had started talking about war, when Lee had only been worrying about a single opponent. That reminded Lee of a book he had upstairs in his room, *A Book of Five Rings*, written by a famous samurai warrior, probably the most famous, Musashi. Musashi had fought valiantly in many wars and had been undefeated in over sixty duels with swords. He said strategy was the same whether you fought by yourself or with an army. Maybe there was some strategy in Musashi's book that could help Lee now.

Lee ate his dinner as fast as he could and ran upstairs to his room. He had two single beds lined up against one wall with a narrow table in between. Both beds had plaid spreads and bolster pillows to make them look like couches during the day. Lee's huge desk, which had once been in his dad's office, had been painted blue and covered with a Formica surface.

Above the desk, mounted on the wall, were bookshelves filled with books about karate, martial arts, stacks of comic books from his mother's company, and biographies of famous military commanders like Napoleon, Alexander the Great, and Ulysses S. Grant. Lee wasn't sure he wanted to join the army someday, like his father had, but he'd always enjoyed reading about famous military campaigns.

Lee's favorite book, though, was Musashi's. Not only was Musashi the greatest warrior who ever lived, but there were a lot of similarities between Musashi's life and Lee's. Musashi, who was born in Japan in 1584, was orphaned by the time he was seven and sent to live with his uncle, a priest. Lee, too, remembered what it was like to be an orphan and taken in by another family. Musashi was a master of Kendo, the art of the sword. That was why Lee had chosen the sai as his weapon. When he was twirling and jabbing with the two short swords, he liked to imagine that he was doing and feeling the same things Musashi did.

What was even more interesting to Lee right now, though, was that Musashi had slain his first opponent when he was only thirteen. Lee had just turned twelve, but that wasn't so much younger. Of course, Lee would never kill someone, as Musashi did, but there had to be something in *A Book of Five Rings* that would help Lee figure out what to do about the Whittakers.

Reaching up to the lowest bookshelf, Lee pulled down a slim beige hardcover book. The illustration on the front showed a black and red drawing of Musashi, his two swords extended above his head. Lee flipped through the pages, and a passage in the introduction caught his eye:

> . . . *cut the opponent just as he cuts you. This is the ultimate timing . . . it is lack of anger. It means to treat your enemy as an honoured guest.*

Did that mean Lee couldn't even feel angry at Kevin and Jason for the way they were acting? That didn't sound right. That was even worse than not being able to fight them.

Flipping further, Lee found another passage that totally contradicted the first:

> *This is a truth: when you sacrifice your life, you must make fullest use of your weaponry. It is false not to do so, and to die with a weapon yet undrawn.*

Lee knew this meant you had to fight to the finish, no matter what, without fear.

So where did that leave him, Lee wondered, sinking into his desk chair. Was he supposed to invite Kevin and Jason over for a game of catch, or run them through with his sai? Lee closed the book slowly and felt his eyes lose focus as he stared at nothing. He still hadn't found an answer. If anything, he was even more confused than he was before.

Chapter Six

"Your front tire looks as good as new," Jeremy said to Lee as they unlocked their bicycles the next day after school. "It's a good thing we had a spare in the garage."

"We'd just better hope Kevin doesn't get slash happy again," Lee said glumly as he threw his bicycle lock into his knapsack. He looked around for Michael, who usually met them here so they could all go to the dojo together. "Where's Michael?" he asked Jeremy.

Jeremy shrugged. "How should I know? I haven't spoken to him all day. He must have already left for karate class."

"But we always go together," Lee said.

"He probably didn't want to walk with me," Jeremy said. "And that's fine with me because I don't want to walk with him, either."

"I wish you two would knock it off," Lee said. "It's a stupid fight and all it's doing is tearing us apart when we should be sticking together."

"Shhhh!" Jeremy said suddenly, staring up the grassy hill at the football field. "Look!"

Lee followed Jeremy's gaze and felt his stomach start to churn. Jason Whittaker, dressed for football practice in his helmet, shoulder pads, and red and white football jersey, was throwing footballs at a black rubber tire suspended by a rope from a wooden scaffold. He was aiming at the hole in the tire, trying to shoot through the center, but his last ball hit the rim and bounced off onto the short, dry grass.

As the ball landed, Kevin Whittaker, who was standing near the tire, skittered forward to grab the ball. Then he picked it up and hurled it awkwardly at his brother, the ball landing several yards short of Jason's feet.

"Sorry!" Kevin called, running awkwardly back to his position.

"What a klutz!" Jeremy said to Lee, with a triumphant grin. "He's not going to be another Jason, that's for sure."

Lee nodded in agreement. Kevin was so clumsy with the ball and so apologetic about it that Lee almost felt sorry for him. But then Lee remembered who he was feeling sorry for and the feeling vanished.

"Come on, Whittaker!" called the deep, gruff voice of an older man. Lee saw Coach Ryan sitting on the bottom row of bleachers, not far from where Jason was standing. He was balding, and his stomach was so big it looked like he'd swallowed a basketball.

Jason took another football from a basket nearby and held it near his shoulder for a second as he focused on the tire. Then he launched it and the ball sailed through the air in a graceful arc—missing the tire completely.

"That's the fifth one in a row you've missed," Coach Ryan said irritably. "And you've been off in practice, too. What's the matter with you?"

Lee couldn't hear Jason's reply, but he saw Jason's helmeted head droop forward.

"You're losing it," Coach Ryan warned. "You're looking like an old man out there."

"I'm just a little tired," Jason said, and he sounded it.

"Well, wake up!" Coach Ryan said, getting up off the bleacher. "We've got a big game tomorrow. We're counting on you." He took a red baseball cap out of the back pocket of his pants and shoved it on his head. "I'm going to round up the rest of the team," he said. "Meanwhile, I want you to throw a hundred more of those." He headed down the hill, past Lee and Jeremy, toward the back entrance to the gymnasium.

Jason grabbed a football from the basket and spiked it hard, into the ground. It bounced up again so fast it reminded Lee of a rocket taking off. Then Kevin pointed at Lee and shouted, "There he is!"

Though Lee wanted to avoid contact with the Whittakers as much as possible, he wasn't going to run away, either. He stood motionless by his bike as Kevin ran down the hill, followed by Jason. Musashi's words echoed in his ears. A true samurai faced danger as if it were routine.

"*He's* the one who did it," said Kevin, pointing at Lee. "He's the one who slashed my tires."

Lee felt like he'd been hit in the face. It was one thing to face danger. It was another to face an outright lie. "What?" Lee shouted at Kevin. "What are you talking about?"

Jason, still holding a football, jumped the last few feet down the hill and landed on the pavement. Then he took off his helmet and his eyes flashed with anger. "You can't call my brother a liar this time," he said. "I saw what you did to Kevin's bike. Well, I'll tell you something, punk, one way or another you're gonna pay for it. Know what I mean?"

"I didn't touch his bike," Lee said. "I'm the one

whose tire got slashed." The injustice of it all made him feel sick. And furious.

Now Jason looked pointedly at Lee's bike, with its nice, new spare. "Yeah, right, tell me another," he muttered.

"It's true," Lee insisted. "Kevin lies, and you believe him!" He could hardly believe what was happening, but as soon as the words were out of his mouth, he knew he'd made everything worse.

Jason's face darkened like a thundercloud. "I told you to leave my brother alone," he said. "I told you not to call him a liar. But you wouldn't listen. Now I'm gonna make you listen. In fact, I'm gonna pound it into you." He handed the football and helmet to Kevin.

"Come on, Jenkins, let's get it over with," Jason said.

"He won't fight you," Kevin said, laughing meanly. "He's too chicken."

"Oh yeah?" Jason said. "Is that so?"

Lee's fists were clenching and unclenching, and his palms were sweating. He was so close to leaping at Jason he had to use every last bit of his self-control to make his feet to stick to the ground. Jeremy, standing beside him, holding up his bike, was beginning to turn a bright shade of red.

"I'm tired of waiting, Jenkins," Jason said, impatiently tapping the toe of his spiked football shoe. "I'm getting bored. I hate being bored."

Lee willed his face to show no emotion. Jeremy, on the other hand, was starting to breathe heavily.

"Come on, karate boy," Jason said, waving his fingers in Lee's face. "Throw the first punch. That's all I ask. Throw the first punch."

"You know I can't do that," Lee said.

"I know!" Jason said gleefully. "You karate people hate to do that. That's why I want you to. Come on, just one little punch!" Jason held up his fists like a boxer and began to dance around on his spikes.

"No!" Lee insisted as Jason danced closer and closer. "I won't do it."

"Then I will!" Jeremy screamed, lunging forward. *"Hyyyaaaaahhhhhh!"* He gave a thundering kiai and landed a solid kick right in the middle of Jason's stomach.

Jason staggered back a step, then aimed a right hook at Jeremy's face. Jeremy tried to block, but Jason was too quick. Jason's punch hit hard, on the side of his head, sending Jeremy's glasses flying through the air. They landed on the pavement with a crash. Then Jason followed with a left to Jeremy's mouth. Jeremy reeled and stumbled to the ground, a trickle of blood coming out of the side of his mouth.

Lee ran to Jeremy and knelt down. "What did he do to you?" Lee cried.

"Not as much as I'm going to do," Jason jeered, still dancing around on the pavement with his fists up. "Unless you want to stop me. Get up and fight, chicken!"

Lee ignored Jason. He wanted to make sure Jeremy was okay. Lee watched as Jeremy touched his fingers to his mouth and pulled them away bright red with blood.

"Any loose teeth?" Lee asked.

Jeremy shook his head. "I'm okay," he said. "I'm just really mad at myself that I got him in the stomach instead of the solar plexus. If I'd only kicked a few inches higher . . ."

"Don't worry about that now," Lee said. "Does anything hurt?"

"My head doesn't feel too great," Jeremy said, "and I can't see too well without my glasses."

Lee looked around for Jeremy's glasses and found them lying on the pavement, a few feet away. One lens was completely shattered, and the other one was cracked.

"Here," Lee said, handing Jeremy his glasses, "this will be better than nothing." Then Lee turned to face

Jason who stood there smirking. Lee had held out as long as he could, but now he'd reached the breaking point. Jason had injured his brother and was ready for more. It would be wrong for Lee *not* to fight back and protect them both. Lee was relieved that the choice had finally become clear.

"Okay," Lee said quietly. "You want a fight? You've got it."

Jason smiled, and his green eyes narrowed into slits. "It's about time! Come on, karate boy, give me your best shot."

Lee turned his body to the side and crouched low, ready to attack.

"Hey, hey, what's going on here?"

Lee, Jeremy, and Jason turned and saw Coach Ryan returning from the gym, several football players behind him.

"Uh . . . nothing, Coach," Jason said, leaning down to pick up his helmet. "The ball flew over here, and when I came to get it, I found these two kids fighting."

Kids? Lee bristled at the word. Jason was only a year older than he was, even if he *was* in eighth grade.

"Is that true?" Coach Ryan asked Lee.

Lee felt torn. If he told Coach Ryan the truth, then he and Jeremy would get in trouble for fighting and Jason might get suspended from the football team.

Then the whole school would be mad at him. Worst of all, he'd be telling. Like a baby who couldn't solve his own problems. Besides, why should the coach believe him? No, Lee couldn't tell the coach the truth.

If he went along with Jason's story, he could still get his revenge on Jason—later. But he didn't want the coach to think he and Jeremy were fighting either.

"Actually," Lee said, "my brother just fell off his bicycle and broke his glasses."

Coach Ryan crossed his thick arms over his chest and looked at Lee like he didn't believe him.

"That's really what happened, Coach," Jeremy said, sitting up and putting on his broken glasses. "We weren't fighting."

Jason grabbed the football back from Kevin. "Well, Coach," he said, "I guess I'd better get back to practice. I still have ninety-four more passes to throw."

Coach Ryan shook his head and pressed his lips together. "I know I'm not getting the whole story," he said, "but I'll let it slide, *this time*. If I ever catch any of you fighting again, though . . ."

Jason nodded in agreement. "You'd better listen to him, you guys. Don't mess with the Coach-man." He let Coach Ryan start up the hill ahead of him. When the coach was out of hearing range, Jason turned back to Lee with a nasty expression. "Don't think this is the end of it," he said in a low voice. "We're going to finish this. Soon." Then, without even looking at Lee or Jeremy, he sprinted up the hill back toward the football field, Kevin trailing behind him like a shadow.

Lee stared at them as they walked away, his heart still pounding hard.

A little wobbly, Jeremy rose to his feet. "Thanks for trying to defend me," he said. "I know you really didn't want to fight him."

"What you did was stupid, Jeremy," Lee said, "but I couldn't let him hurt you even more."

"And what if Jason tries again?" Jeremy questioned him.

"I don't know," Lee said. "It's one thing to defend yourself when the fight's already started, but I don't know what's going to happen next time."

"So what are you going to do?" Jeremy asked.

Lee inhaled deeply and sighed. "The only thing I can think of," he said. "I'm going to talk to the sensei."

Chapter Seven

Poing!

The dojo was quiet and still. It was so quiet that Michael could hear drops of water fall from the leaking ceiling into a bucket at the other end of the long room. *Poing!* Sensei was always having trouble with leaky pipes.

It was the end of karate class and Michael sat on the floor in seiza position, eyes closed, hands crossed in his lap. He knew his mind was supposed to be blank, but it kept filling with questions. Where were Lee and Jeremy? Why hadn't they come to class? Kevin Whittaker hadn't shown up either. Was there a connection?

Poing! Another drop fell in the bucket. Michael tried to tune out the noise and his thoughts, but he couldn't stop worrying about his brothers. They *never* missed karate. Something bad must have happened to them. Could that something be Jason Whittaker?

Sensei Davis clapped his hands and the white-uniformed boys and girls jumped to their feet. "Arigato, Sensei!" they shouted.

"Arigato," the sensei said, bowing. "Volunteers to sweep the deck?"

Eleven pairs of bare feet ran across the wooden floor toward the broom closet at the back of the dojo. Every day, after the 3:30 class was over, the karate students, or *deshi,* would clean the floor. It was just as important to show spirit while pushing a broom as it was to have good karate techniques.

Michael was the first to grab a broom. He swept along the side of the floor, toward the bulletin board where the sensei posted announcements and quotes. As he swept, he thought again about Lee and Jason Whittaker. Lee hadn't done anything to Jason. Lee hadn't really done anything to Kevin either. So why had Kevin taken it so personally when Lee beat him in kumite? Why was he trying so hard to start a fight between Jason and Lee? And what could Michael do to stop it from happening?

Michael looked up at the bulletin board as he swept

past and noticed a new quote, handwritten on an index card, thumbtacked to the cork. The quote said:

The secret of victory is to know both yourself and your enemy.
—*Chinese proverb*

Michael stopped sweeping and stared at the quote. That was it! That was the answer he'd been looking for, or at least the way to *find* the answer. Michael had to *understand* Kevin and Jason. If Michael could figure out *why* they were doing this, maybe he could find a way of stopping it.

But how was he going to do that? Michael couldn't exactly go up to Jason in the lunchroom and say, "Let's get to know each other better, okay?" Jason would probably send him flying across the room. No, there had to be some other way.

What about Suzanne? She was still mad that Jeremy had called her a spy, but she might answer some of Michael's questions. Michael didn't want to wait until the next day in science class to talk to her. He wanted to talk to her *now*. He could get her address from the list of karate students he kept in his locker because her brother Kevin was on the list. Then he could stop at the Whittakers' house on his way home. It was a good thing Kevin Whittaker wasn't in class today or Michael would have to explain to Kevin why he was following him.

Michael swept his pile of dirt into the center of the floor where another deshi knelt with a dustpan and whisk broom. The deshi swept everyone's dirt into the pan and walked it over to a trash can at the rear of the dojo. Michael returned his broom to the closet and ran to the locker room to get dressed. He couldn't wait to put his plan into action.

As Michael rode his bike away from the Midvale Mall, he had a disturbing thought. What if Jason was home when Michael got to the Whittakers' house? He probably wouldn't even let Michael get past the front door. He might even turn Michael into a new doormat. Michael pushed the thought out of his mind. He couldn't worry about that now. He had to help Lee, no matter how risky it was.

Michael turned right onto a street with split level houses. The houses were all brand new and looked almost exactly alike with sloping lawns and few trees. It was hard to tell them apart.

A sign up ahead said Grand Avenue. That was where the Whittakers lived. Michael turned left onto another street that looked exactly like the one he'd just been on. One house up ahead, though, stood out from the others, mainly because its front walk was all torn up. All that was left was a shallow rut snaking across the lawn, leading to the front door. Several big bags of cement were scattered on the lawn. When Michael got closer and checked the address, he realized that this was the Whittakers' house!

Michael parked his bike in the driveway and heard the tinny whine of an electric saw coming from inside the house. Cutting across the lawn, Michael rang the doorbell, but it was impossible to hear anything over the loud noise.

The front door was open, with a screen door behind it. Looking through the screen, Michael saw the back of a large man dressed in overalls, sawing planks of wood over two sawhorses. Behind him, against the wall, was a half-built bookcase.

Michael waited until the sawing stopped. Then he called, "Excuse me. Is Suzanne home?"

The man turned around. Even though clear plastic goggles covered half his face, something about him reminded Michael of Jason. Michael wondered if this man was Jason's father.

"Suzanne!" the man called, turning back to his saw. "Someone's here to see you."

As the deafening whine began again, Suzanne appeared on a second floor balcony overlooking the living room. "What are you doing here?" she asked, running down the short flight of stairs.

"I need to talk to you," Michael said. "It's very important."

Suzanne looked over her shoulder at the living room. "I don't know," she said, nervously pulling on one of her brown curls. "The house is sort of a mess right now."

"I don't care about that," Michael said impatiently. "I just need to talk to you. It's about my brother and Jason."

Suzanne bit her lip. For a second, Michael thought that she was going to tell him to go home, but then she pushed open the screen door. "It's really a mess," Suzanne repeated. "Try not to look."

Michael stepped inside the living room and almost tripped over a metal tool chest. The room smelled like sawdust. Pushed off to one side were several sheet-covered lumps that were probably furniture.

"We can go down to the rec room," Suzanne said. "That's about the only room in the house that's not under construction."

Michael followed Suzanne down another flight of stairs. "Was that your dad up there?" he asked.

"Yeah," Suzanne shouted over the saw.

"Looks like he's a real do-it-yourselfer," Michael said.

Suzanne said nothing as she led Michael into a large wood-paneled room. The room had a long black leather couch, a TV, and a large glass trophy case. Glass doors at the end of the room led out to a backyard.

"Okay," Suzanne said resignedly, crossing her arms. "What do you want?"

She seemed kind of annoyed. "I'm only here because I'm trying to help," Michael said.

"Yeah, right," Suzanne said. "That's what I tried to do, too, and all I got for it was insults from your little brother."

"Jeremy didn't know what he was talking about," Michael said. "He's always shooting off his mouth without thinking. I'm sorry he said you were a spy. I know you were trying to help."

Suzanne sighed and uncrossed her arms. "I still am," she said, sounding a little more friendly. "I tried talking to Jason and Kevin again about calling off the fight, but they're both so stubborn!"

"That's what I wanted to talk to you about," Michael said. "Why are they doing this? What did Lee ever do to them?"

"Nothing," Suzanne said, walking over to the couch and sitting down. "This has nothing to do with Lee."

Suzanne hadn't invited Michael to sit, but he didn't think she'd mind. He sat down on the other end of the couch. "What are you talking about?" he asked. "They're making Lee's life miserable."

Suzanne shrugged. "It's not important."

"It *is* important," Michael insisted. "It could be the clue I'm looking for. I need to know more about your brothers."

Suzanne gestured toward the glass display case. "You can start there," she said.

Michael looked through the glass and saw several shelves filled with shining football trophies. Some were brass footballs sitting on flat bases. Others had a column with football player figurines. There were also plaques with Jason's name under the words "Most Valuable Player."

"Wow!" Michael exclaimed. "I knew he was good, but I didn't know how good."

"He's better than good," Suzanne said. "The high-school football coach has already promised Jason he'll play varsity his sophomore year. The coach even thinks Jason can win a football scholarship to college."

Even though Michael didn't like Jason very much right now, he couldn't help being impressed. But he still didn't see how this answered his question. "What else can you tell me about him?" Michael asked. "And what does this have to do with Kevin?"

Suzanne leaned back on the couch and folded her legs Indian style. "Let's put it this way," she said. "Kevin will never fill up a case like that. And even though Jason could probably fill up ten more, he'll probably have a nervous breakdown before he's through."

"Jason?" Michael asked. "Mr. MVP? What's he got to be nervous about?"

"He's under a lot of pressure right now," Suzanne answered. "He's got the team, of course, and he works really hard after school, too. He mows lawns, rakes leaves, shovels snow. Anything he can think of. He earns almost a hundred dollars a week! He says he's going to be rich some day."

"At that rate, sounds like he will," Michael said. "But if it's too much for him, why doesn't he just slow down?"

Before Suzanne could answer, a pair of sneakered feet appeared on the stairs, followed by long, long legs, the number twelve, and the angry face of Jason Whittaker.

"What is a *Jenkins* doing on *my property?*" Jason demanded.

"It's not your property," Suzanne shot back. "We all live here. I invited him in."

"Well, invite him *out. Now!*" Jason ordered her.

"No!" Suzanne shouted, suddenly furious. "You can't tell me who I can have over to the house. Michael can stay if he wants."

"Well maybe he won't want to stay once he finds out what happened to his brother," Jason jeered. "He's hurting pretty badly right now. Maybe you better run home and see how he is."

"Which brother?" Michael asked, alarmed. "Lee or Jeremy?"

"Maybe both," Jason said, laughing.

"I've got to go," Michael said to Suzanne.

Suzanne shrugged helplessly. Jason mockingly stepped aside as Michael raced past him on the stairs.

What had happened now? Michael hardly dared to think of it as he flew home on his bike.

Chapter Eight

"Are you sure you're going to be able to ride in your condition?" Lee asked Jeremy, helping his brother stand up.

Jeremy peered back at Lee through one cracked lens of his glasses. He'd removed the broken glass from the other lens so all that was left was an empty round frame. "Sure I can ride," Jeremy said. "Jason broke my glasses, not my legs."

"Yeah, but you might not be able to see too well when we're riding on the street," Lee said. "Maybe we'd better walk on the sidewalk."

"We've spent enough time walking our bikes, thanks to the Whittakers," Jeremy said, stiffening. "I'm not letting them ground us again. I'll be okay. We'll just take it slow, and I'll follow you."

Lee straddled his bicycle. "Okay, but be careful,"

he warned. He started pedaling slowly along the cement path behind the school, checking over his shoulder every few seconds.

"I'm not that blind!" Jeremy called out, pedaling behind Lee. "Just watch the road!"

Lee turned left at the chain link fence and started up the hill.

"Hey! Where are you going?" Jeremy yelled. "The dojo's the other way!"

"We're going home," Lee called over his shoulder.

"But we'll miss karate class!" Jeremy protested.

"We can miss one class," Lee told him. "We'll talk about it when we get home, okay?"

When Lee got to the top of the hill, he crossed over a main road then around a curving road past the Bonny Brook Country Club. Then he turned left onto a wide, tree-lined street. The road narrowed and twisted and became a dead end.

At the end of the road, partially hidden behind bushes and trees, was the Jenkins house. It was an old, stone house, built into a hill, with a woods behind it. A slate path led from the door across the lawn down three steps to the street.

Checking again over his shoulder to make sure Jeremy was still behind him, Lee turned into the driveway.

Both garage doors were still closed, which meant that neither of his parents was home yet. Lee hopped off his bike and pulled out a chain from under his shirt. The chain had two keys on it: a larger one for the front door and a smaller one for the electronic garage. Lee put the smaller one in a lock by the garage door and turned it. Obediently, the door began to slide up out of sight. Lee parked his bike and waited while Jeremy rode into the garage.

"Let me get something to put on your mouth," Lee said as they opened the door that led into the kitchen.

"I don't have time for that," Jeremy told him. "I'm going upstairs to get my spare glasses. You may think it's okay to miss class, but I don't."

Lee faced Jeremy squarely. "Look in the mirror, okay?"

Jeremy stared at him a minute, then walked into the hall. There was a large mirror hanging over a table near the stairway. Lee watched as Jeremy went over and looked at what had happened to his face. His mouth was very swollen on one side, his lip cut and puffy. A purplish bruise was emerging along his jaw.

"Wow," was all Jeremy could say.

Lee came out and stood next to him. "If we put some ice on it, maybe the swelling will go down. Aside from the fact that I really think you should take it easy, think about what mom and dad will say. The best thing we can do is try to make you look as good as possible."

"Wrong," Jeremy said.

Lee braced himself. He didn't want to fight with his brother, but he really didn't want him to leave the house. How could he convince Jeremy to stay?

"The best thing we can do is to make me look as un-bad as possible," Jeremy continued wryly.

"Come on," Lee said, relieved that Jeremy finally agreed with him. "Let's get some ice."

Back in the kitchen, Lee tore some paper towels off the roll above the sink while Jeremy sat at the kitchen table. Then Lee pulled a handful of ice cubes out of the freezer and wrapped them in the paper towels.

"Here," he said, handing the wad to Jeremy. "Put this on your mouth." He sat down at the table across from his brother and put his head in his hands. He felt terrible. None of this ever would have happened if it hadn't been for him. It was all his fault.

Jeremy held the ice cubes to his mouth and sighed. "Haseesoogogradee," he said through the ice cubes, the paper towels, and his swollen lip.

"What?" Lee asked.

93

Jeremy took the ice cubes away from his mouth. "At least *you* should go to karate," he repeated. "There's no reason why you should miss it."

"It's almost over by now," Lee said. "I'd get there too late. Besides, I should stay with you."

"I don't need a babysitter," Jeremy said, offended. "And you said you were going to talk to the sensei. So go!"

"Do you promise you won't try to follow me?" Lee asked. "You'll stay home?"

"I promise," Jeremy said. "Like you said, class is almost over anyway. I'm just going to go upstairs and get my old glasses. Then I'll watch TV or start my homework or something."

"Okay," Lee said. "I'll be back soon."

Lee headed back for the garage and hopped on his bike. Then he pedaled as fast as he could back down the street. He knew class would be over by the time he reached the dojo, but there was nothing he could do about that now. It was much more important that he talk to Sensei before the evening class started.

Lee had thought he could solve the Jason problem on his own, but it wasn't working out that way. If anything, he was *more* uncertain. Jason had hurt Jeremy. Did that mean Lee was justified in going after Jason now? Or did he have to wait until Jason tried

94

to hurt him or his brothers again? The sensei had to have the answer.

The bike rack outside the dojo was empty. That meant class was already over. Lee hoped the sensei was still around. Lee quickly locked his bike and tried the door. It was open. Good. The sensei must be around somewhere.

The front hall was empty and the door to the sensei's office was closed. Lee peered through the window leading to the classroom and breathed a sigh of relief. The sensei was there, alone, practicing a *kata*.

A kata was a series of moves—blocks, punches, and kicks—performed against imaginary opponents coming from all directions. Kata had to be practiced over and over, hundreds and thousands of times, so that the moves became instinctive. The kata the sensei practiced now was the most basic kata with low blocks, high blocks, and walking punches.

Lee stared through the glass as Sensei Davis practiced at half speed and power. Though the sensei's movements were slow and graceful, Lee could also see how much power the sensei had. His arms and legs looked as thick and sturdy as tree trunks.

As Lee watched, though, he began to wonder why anyone studied martial arts in the first place. Here was the sensei, a third degree black belt, pretending to fight invisible opponents. Was that all karate was for? Was it just to use perfect techniques on enemies who weren't even there? And to prevent you from fighting real ones?

The sensei finished his kata and bowed. Then, without turning around, he said, "What can I do for you, Lee?" Lee was startled. The sensei hadn't seemed to notice Lee while he was doing kata. But then Lee remembered what his sensei always said. You had to be aware of everything around you, even while you were focused on something else.

"Onegai-shimasu, Sensei," Lee said, stepping into the doorway and bowing. Please teach me, Sensei.

Sensei Davis turned to face Lee. "Onegai-shimasu," he said. "Wait there."

Bowing to the photographs of the karate masters, the sensei pushed aside the curtain leading from the deck to his office and disappeared inside. Seconds later, he opened the office door leading to the hall where Lee was standing.

"Come in," the sensei said.

Lee entered the office uncertainly.

"Sit down, Lee," the sensei invited him, seating himself behind his battered desk.

Lee sat in the straight-backed wooden chair and looked down at his hands. Then he looked up at the sensei, who waited patiently, his dark brown eyes calm.

"I couldn't solve my problem," Lee began. "That's why I wasn't in class today. Well, actually, my problem came looking for me."

"Your problem has legs?" the sensei asked, folding his hands across the sweaty, faded black belt tied around his waist.

"Two of them," Lee said. "Two big, thick legs, and an even thicker head on top."

The sensei raised his sandy colored eyebrows. "I see. Was it someone from the dojo?"

"Yes and no," Lee said. "I mean, it started out that way but now so many people have gotten involved I don't know where to start."

"Take your time," the sensei said.

As clearly as he could, Lee explained the situation, starting with Kevin and kumite, then Jason, Michael and Suzanne, Michael's fight with Jeremy, and ending with Jeremy's fight with Jason.

"And I don't know what to do now," Lee concluded. "I mean, it was the right thing to defend my brother today, wasn't it?"

"That was correct," the sensei said. "Defending a member of your family is like defending yourself. The rules are the same."

"But what do I do now?" Lee asked. "Would it still be correct for me to go after Jason now? Or do I have to act like a sitting duck until he decides to come after me again?"

"Let me tell you a story," Sensei said, leaning forward on his desk. "Many years ago, a great karate master was approached by a student. The student said, 'Master, you have spent your life studying karate. You are the most powerful fighter in all the land. Students come from hundreds of miles to learn from you. What would you do if you were alone on the street and a large man threatened to attack you?'

"The great karate master replied 'I would run.'

" 'Run, Master?' asked the surprised student. 'But there is no one stronger than you.'

"To this, the Master nodded and said 'I would run with confidence.' "

Sensei Davis leaned back in his chair and stroked his sandy colored mustache with one finger.

Lee knew the sensei's answer was hidden in the story. "Are you saying we should never fight, no matter how advanced we get in karate?" Lee asked.

The sensei shook his head. "You missed a key

word," he said. "The word was *threatened*. If the large man had *threatened* to attack, the Master would have run to avoid fighting, which is always the first choice. Threats are just words."

Lee nodded. The sensei's meaning was becoming clear. "But if the man had raised his fist to strike a blow, that would have been different, right?"

Sensei Davis nodded. "That is the only time you are permitted to use your techniques—to block the attack."

"And if he keeps on attacking?" Lee asked.

"Then you may use whatever force is necessary to disable your opponent."

"But what if he's attacked you in the past?" Lee asked. "Is that a good enough reason to strike back?"

"No," the sensei said. "That fight is over already. If you went after him now, that wouldn't be self-defense. That would be revenge."

"So where does that leave me?" Lee asked.

The sensei smiled. "Without a problem. So far, you've handled each situation correctly. You've avoided fighting when Jason threatened you and stepped in only to defend your brother. Have confidence in your training and your instincts."

Lee sighed in relief. "So I'm not a sitting duck?"

"Far from it," the sensei said. "Don't wait for Jason

to act or not act. Just live your life as if he doesn't exist. And if your paths should cross again, you'll know what to do."

Lee smiled. Knowing the sensei had confidence in him gave him more confidence in himself. And knowing he'd done well so far made him feel like he could handle anything else that happened.

Lee stood up. "Arigato, Sensei!" he said, bowing.

"Arigato," Sensei Davis said.

Lee left the dojo and bicycled home, feeling more peaceful than he had in days.

Chapter Nine

Michael hunched forward over the handlebars of his bike and rode home like he was trying to win a race. As he rounded the curve past the Bonny Brook Country Club, his legs churned like pistons. Up ahead, pedaling almost as fast, was a smaller boy with straight black hair on a red ten-speed bicycle. Since Michael wasn't expecting to see Lee in one piece, Michael almost passed him before he realized who it was.

"Lee!" Michael exclaimed, slowing down to keep pace with his brother. "What happened today? I was so worried when you and Jeremy didn't show up for class, and then I ran into Jason Whittaker . . ."

"You might say Jeremy tried to take a flying leap through Jason's stomach . . . ," Lee began, "which didn't thrill Jason too much." As Lee and Michael

101

turned onto their street, Lee filled in the rest of what had happened after school. "But how did you run into Jason?" Lee asked. "Did he come to the dojo?"

Before Michael could answer, they reached their house and saw that both their mother's sportscar and their father's Jeep were in the garage.

"Uh-oh," Lee said.

"I'll tell you later," Michael said as they coasted into the garage and jumped off their bicycles. Before they'd even opened the door to the kitchen, they could hear loud voices inside the house.

"Did you see what he did to my baby?" Mrs. Jenkins was yelling at her husband as Lee and Michael entered the kitchen. "Let me at that little creep. I'll punch him out myself!"

"I'm not a baby," Jeremy said thickly through his swollen lip. He slumped in a chair at the table, wearing his old, brown, horn-rimmed glasses with a piece of masking tape wrapped around the middle to hold the frame together. "And Jason's not so little. He's at least half a foot taller than you and about fifty pounds heavier."

"Don't underestimate me," his mother said, pacing rapidly back and forth across the blue and white linoleum floor in her black high heels. She kept running her fingers through her copper-colored hair, so that it stood out farther and farther away from her head. Mr. Jenkins stood glumly by the stove, stirring spaghetti sauce.

"Most bullies are all talk and no action," Mr. Jenkins observed, "and if Jeremy hadn't made the first move, maybe nothing would have happened."

"You *told* them?" Michael asked Jeremy. He hadn't expected Jeremy to admit the truth to his parents.

Jeremy shrugged. "I'm not ashamed of what I did," he said. "I was fed up."

"And so am I," Mrs. Jenkins declared, marching over to the light blue wall phone. "I'm calling Jason's parents right now."

"Mo-o-o-om!" Jeremy wailed, jumping up and trying to grab the phone before she did. "You can't call Jason's parents. I'll look like a total baby!"

"If you want to worry about what you look like, look in the mirror," Mrs. Jenkins said. "That fat lip he gave you makes you look worse than anything I'm going to do." She picked up the receiver and punched out the number for information.

"But you don't understand!" Jeremy pleaded. "It's bad enough Jason beat me up. You don't want kids at school to think I'm a sissy, do you?"

"You're not a sissy," Mrs. Jenkins argued. "You

gave him what he was asking for. Now I'm going to do the same. Does anybody know what street that creep lives on?"

"Grand Avenue," Michael said quietly.

Lee and Jeremy turned to Michael in surprise while his mother dialed information.

"How did you know that?" Jeremy asked in a nasty tone. "Did you go over to the Whittakers' to visit your *girlfriend,* Suzanne?"

Michael was surprised for a moment at Jeremy's attitude. Michael had been so concerned for Jeremy's safety that he'd forgotten they weren't speaking to each other. But Jeremy's tone brought it all back.

"For your information . . . ," he began, but his mother interrupted him. She'd gotten the number and had dialed the Whittakers.

"Shhhh!" she hushed them, waving her hand. "It's ringing."

Jeremy pressed down the button on the phone. "For the last time mom, *no.* Butt out. Please?"

Mr. Jenkins poured a box of spaghetti into a big pot of boiling water. "We did," he said, "and look what happened. Why couldn't you tell us what was going on? We would have understood. We would have tried to help you."

Jeremy rolled his eyes. "Somehow, the idea of my

mother punching out Jason Whittaker doesn't strike me as help."

Lee checked the duty roster on the refrigerator, then went over to the cabinet where dishes were stored. "That's not the kind of help dad's talking about, Jeremy. They're a lot older than us. Like Sensei Davis. They know things we don't." He carried a stack of plates over to the table and began setting places.

"I'm not *that* old," his mother protested. She pulled a long, skinny loaf of Italian bread out of a long white bag and began slicing it. "But I don't understand why you don't want me to call. When I was a little girl, and the tough kids would pick on me, all my mother would say was 'In life, you've got to learn to fight your own battles.' I used to be so scared I'd stay in my pajamas in the house all weekend."

"Yes, but you did learn," Mr. Jenkins said. "Now you can stand up to anybody."

"That's right," Mrs. Jenkins said proudly.

"Don't you want your sons to grow up the same way?"

Mrs. Jenkins started slicing the Italian bread more slowly. "I never thought of that," she said thoughtfully. "I just promised myself I'd stand up for my kids."

"But that's not what *I* want," Jeremy said.

"How about you?" Mrs. Jenkins asked Lee and Michael. "Do you want me to stay out of it?"

Lee and Michael nodded yes. For the first time in two days, Jeremy smiled at Michael.

Mrs. Jenkins sighed and shrugged her shoulders. "I guess I'm overruled," she said.

"Who's hungry for spaghetti?" Mr. Jenkins asked, pouring the steaming pot of spaghetti into a colander in the sink.

"I am!" said everyone.

Lee sat at the end of Michael's bed, tossing spongy orange balls into a plastic basketball hoop mounted above the headboard. He easily sank shot after shot, pausing only to pick up the balls from the floor. It felt so good to be in control again, to know what he had to do. And it was all because he'd spoken to the sensei.

Lee wished, now, that he'd said something sooner rather than wait until things got so out of hand. Now if only Lee could get his brothers to start speaking to each other again, most of his problems would be solved. They'd smiled once at each other, before dinner, but they hadn't spoken a word since.

"Jeremy's lip looks pretty bad," Lee said to Michael, hoping this would make his brother feel some sympathy for Jeremy. In a way, this was cheating since Lee knew Michael was very softhearted, but Lee was desperate to patch things up. He couldn't stand the silences anymore.

Michael didn't seem to hear Lee. He sat at his desk with his magic markers, drawing a very professional looking picture of Turbotron. Turbotron was a superhero their mother had created for Rocket Comics. Turbotron had the mind of a computer, the heart of a man, and superhuman power that came from his internal turbo-charged engine. In the year since she'd created him, Turbotron had become very popular, and Mrs. Jenkins had even been interviewed on talk shows about him. Sometimes Mrs. Jenkins got ideas for Turbotron's adventures from things that happened to Lee, Michael, and Jeremy.

More framed pictures of Turbotron covered the walls of Michael's room, some drawn by Michael, others by the cartoonists at Rocket Comics. Lee found it hard to tell the difference. Michael was definitely going to be a famous cartoonist someday.

"I wonder if Mom and Dad should have taken Jeremy to the hospital," Lee said, pushing it a little. "Maybe he needs stitches."

Michael put down the gray magic marker he was using to shade Turbotron's steel-plated body. "I know

107

what you're doing, Lee," he said. "But don't bother. I'm tired of fighting with Jeremy, anyway."

At that moment, there was a knock at the door. Jeremy opened the door a crack and poked his head in. "Can I come in?" he asked.

Michael nodded. "I was going to come talk to you," he said.

"You were?" Jeremy asked hopefully. "You're not mad at me anymore?"

"I thought *you* were mad at *me,*" Michael said, "for talking to Suzanne. And she's *not* my girlfriend, by the way."

"I'm sorry I said that," Jeremy told him. "But you can see my point, can't you? I mean, she *is* Jason's sister."

"You shouldn't lump them together just because they come from the same family," Michael said. "Just because Kevin and Jason are jerks doesn't mean Suzanne is too. You and I aren't exactly alike, you know."

"Tell me about it," Lee said, tossing another ball at the hoop. It bounced off the backboard and landed at Michael's feet. "If you were, you two wouldn't be having this fight."

"*Are* we?" Michael asked Jeremy.

"Are we what?" Jeremy asked.

"Having this fight," Michael said. "Jason's the enemy, not you or me." He picked up the ball and tossed it at the hoop. It went through and rolled toward Jeremy.

Jeremy picked up the ball and threw it to Michael. "I'll call a truce if you will," he said.

Michael caught the ball. "It's a deal," he said.

Lee breathed a sigh of relief. Maybe things were going to be okay after all. Then his stomach lurched as he remembered he still had unfinished business with Jason Whittaker. Michael had said he'd run into Jason this afternoon, but he hadn't said where. And how had Michael known where the Whittakers lived?

"Where were you this afternoon?" Lee asked Michael, though he was already beginning to guess.

"The Whittakers'," Michael said, confirming Lee's suspicions.

"What?" Jeremy exclaimed, his eyes growing round. "Why did you go there?"

Michael told them about the quote on the sensei's bulletin board. "I thought if I could understand why Jason acts the way he does, it might help Lee," Michael explained. "If the greatest victory is to win without fighting, and the secret to victory is knowing your enemy, then it seems like the way to avoid a fight is to know your enemy."

"Very logical," Jeremy said. "So what did you find out?"

"Well, not as much as I wanted to since Jason walked in before I was finished," Michael said, "but I saw all his football trophies, and his sister told me a lot of things I didn't know." Michael told his brothers about how the Whittakers' house had been all topsy turvy with construction, and how overworked Jason was.

"I don't see how knowing that is going to prevent a fight," Jeremy said. "And what does that have to do with Lee?"

"I don't know," Michael admitted. "I guess I'm not much of a detective."

"Well, thanks for trying," Lee said, "but I've already made up my mind. If Jason wants a fight, he'll have one. Sensei Davis said it's okay."

"Yay!" Jeremy shouted, raising his fist in the air.

Michael looked at Lee in surprise. "The *sensei* said you should fight? But what about *karate ni sente nashi*—there is no first attack in karate?"

"He didn't say I should *start* a fight," Lee said. "He just said that I shouldn't avoid Jason either. And if Jason lays a hand on me, or either of you, I can do whatever's necessary to defend us." Lee picked up a puffy orange ball in his left hand and punched it with his right.

"Oh," Michael said. "I thought he changed the rules on us."

"The rules never change," Lee said confidently.

"Well, if you want to 'not avoid' Jason, you'll have your chance tomorrow at the football game," Jeremy said. "You *know* Jason will be there."

"That's exactly what I was thinking," Lee said. "We always go to the Friday game. Tomorrow's not going to be any different."

"So what are you going to do?" Michael asked. "Just wait until he sees you?"

"No," Lee answered. "I'm just going to do what I'd normally do. And if I *happen* to run into him, and he *happens* to throw the first punch, I'll be ready."

"So will I!" Jeremy exclaimed, slapping Lee on the back. "If you need help, I'll be right beside you."

Michael looked from Lee to Jeremy and back to Lee again. Then he said quietly, "So will I."

Chapter Ten

The crowd was screaming so loud Lee had to stick his fingers in his ears. It was the fourth quarter, and the Dragons were ahead 24 to 20, thanks mostly to Jason Whittaker. He'd thrown for two touchdowns and run for one.

But now, with the clock stopped at five seconds, the Warriors were on the three-yard line and pushing for the go-ahead touchdown. If they succeeded, they'd win the game, and no one from Midvale liked that idea.

"DE-FENSE DE-FENSE!" yelled Michael and Jeremy and several hundred other people.

"HOLD THAT LINE!" cried people all around them.

Though everyone around him was shouting about the game, Lee was more excited and nervous about what might happen *after* the game. Now that he'd made up his mind to fight Jason if necessary, he almost hoped he'd have the chance to do it.

Not that he wasn't scared. He hadn't slept very well last night, wondering whether his karate would really give him a shot at beating Jason. The only place he'd ever used karate was in the dojo. He'd never had to use it in a real fight before.

"JA-SON! JA-SON! JA-SON!" shouted a hoarse voice nearby.

A few rows below him, Lee saw a heavyset man in paint-spattered jeans and a red tee-shirt with the number twelve, Jason's number. The man was screaming so loud his voice was practically gone. Then Lee noticed Kevin and Suzanne sitting on either side of him.

Lee turned to Michael. "Is that—?"

Michael nodded. "Mr. Whittaker."

They turned to watch the game. As the Dragons and the Warriors lined up at the three yard line, Lee was able to pick out Jason in the row of red and white uniforms. Jason was playing linebacker, and though Lee couldn't see his face, Lee knew it wore a ferocious expression as Jason faced the purple-and-gold-uniformed Warriors. It was the same expression Lee had seen yesterday when he and Jason faced off.

113

The clock started ticking again as the Warriors' center snapped the ball to his quarterback. The Warriors' quarterback handed off the ball to one of his running backs, who went wide on a sweep right toward the goal line.

"Oh no!" Jeremy shouted. "He's gonna do it!"

Everyone jumped up in horror to watch the Dragons' sure defeat.

Then, out of nowhere, Jason Whittaker broke through the line, shoved a blocker aside, and tackled the running back, bringing him down just inches away from the goal line as the clock flashed zero seconds.

The Midvale crowd roared. "JA-SON! JA-SON! JA-SON!"

Even Lee got swept up in the excitement, forgetting for a moment that his school's hero was also his worst enemy.

Jason's father leapt out of his seat, screaming at the top of his lungs and pumping his fist in the air. He ran onto the field, straight toward his son, followed by Kevin and Suzanne. The rest of the crowd also rushed down to the field to surround Jason and his teammates.

Lee remained behind, thinking. Something about Jason didn't make sense. Here he was, the star of the team. He was one of the most popular guys in school.

Even now, his fans were lifting him up on their shoulders and carrying him off the field to the locker room.

So why did Jason let his little brother talk him into fighting people he didn't even kow? Why had he lashed out at Lee and Jeremy yesterday when Kevin was telling such an obvious lie? And, of course, the biggest question was—what would happen when Lee and Jason faced each other again?

"Earth to Lee," Jeremy called from the field. "The game's over."

"I know," Lee said, climbing down the nearly empty wooden bleachers. "I was just thinking . . ."

"About the fight?" Michael asked. "Maybe Jason won't even see you with all these people hanging around."

"I'm not worried about that," Lee said. "I was just wondering about Jason . . ."

"Don't waste your time," Jeremy said, when Lee joined his brothers. "We've spent way too much time thinking about him already."

"So what are you going to do now?" Michael asked.

"What we always do after a game," Lee said. "We're going to go hang out on the field with everybody."

"Even if that means running into Jason?" Michael asked.

Lee nodded. "I won't go out of my way to see him, but I'm not gonna hide from him either."

After several minutes, Lee saw Jason come out of the locker room with Coach Ryan. Jason was wearing jeans, sneakers, and his football jersey without the shoulder pads. Kevin followed them, gazing up at his brother adoringly. Mr. Whittaker, too, walked beside them. He looked a little weird wearing the same number on his chest that Jason wore, almost like he was trying to copy Jason. They were like lopsided twins. The coach slapped Jason on the back, then walked away with Mr. Whittaker.

By now, the field was nearly empty except for the Jenkins brothers, Kevin, Jason, and a few other kids hanging around him like he was the King of Midvale. Lee knew he still had a chance to leave before Jason saw him, but he didn't move. Sooner or later he'd have to face up to Jason. It might as well be now.

Across the field, Jason looked up from his fans and saw Lee. Pushing the other kids aside, Jason strode toward Lee like he was coming in for a tackle. "What are you waiting around for?" Jason jeered as he approached. "My autograph?"

"Wow! You can write your name?" Jeremy jeered.

"Nice glasses," Jason snarled. "Especially the tape in the middle. You trying out for *Revenge of the Nerds?*"

"Enough!" Lee said. "You two have already had your fight. This is between Jason and me."

"You should have run away while you still had the chance," Jason said, approaching Lee. "But here you are, and here I am. Guess that means it's time to take care of some unfinished business."

This was it. Lee's imaginary opponent was about to become real. And, much to his amazement, he wasn't nervous like he'd been earlier. His heart was beating at normal speed, his head was clear, his muscles were relaxed. He didn't feel angry or tense.

"I'm ready," Lee said calmly.

Jason held his arms out on either side of him and tilted his head back. "Go ahead," he said. "Punch me, little guy. Take the first shot."

Lee didn't take offense at Jason's insult. It was almost like Lee's mind was somewhere else, in a quiet, peaceful place where words couldn't reach him. "I've already told you I can't do that," Lee said.

"Oh, that's right!" Jason said, putting his palm against his forehead, pretending he'd forgotten.

"You're a karate man. But what are we going to do, then? We don't want my fans to miss the grand finale!"

Lee said nothing but held his ground.

"Okay, have it your way," Jason said. "If the only way you'll fight me is karate-style, then I guess that's what we'll have to do."

Without any warning, Jason then ran at Lee with a fake sounding kiai. "Haaaaa!" he shouted. His leg flew upward, though it was straight and stiff, more like a football kick than a karate kick.

Smoothly, and without thought, Lee stepped to the side. He grabbed Jason's extended leg and yanked it upward, knocking Jason off balance. Jason fell flat on his back to the laughter of the several boys watching. Lee lunged forward into a low stance to follow up with a punch to the nose, but Jason quickly rolled out of the way and jumped to his feet. He held his clenched fists up in front of his face like a boxer, leaving his rib cage exposed.

Seeing an opening, Lee shouted, "I'll show you the *real* way to kick!" and stepped in with a front kick to Jason's short ribs, snapping his leg back instantly, before Jason could grab it. Jason couldn't have grabbed it anyway, though, because he was doubled over, gasping for breath.

"Yay!" Jeremy started to shout, but before the word had left his lips, Jason had straightened up and landed a solid punch in Lee's chest, followed by one to the stomach. Lee tried to block, but the weight of Jason's body gave his punches a force Lee could do little to resist. Lee staggered back. His chest throbbed with pain and his stomach felt queasy, but he was still on his feet.

Jason towered over him, tall and thick like a tree. That's when Lee realized how he could win the fight. He had to chop the tree down. Lee delivered a stinging front snap kick to Jason's thigh, knowing this would cramp Jason's muscle. As Lee had hoped, Jason leaned over to rub his leg, leaving his neck exposed. This was what Lee had been waiting for. Summoning all his energy and power in one big kiai, Lee jumped in with a knife hand to Jason's neck.

"*Hyaaaahhhh!*" Lee kiaied as the side of his hand connected with his target.

Jason toppled over and lay on the ground. He rolled onto his back, his arms at his sides, and almost did look like a fallen tree. His eyes were open, though, and angry. Lee knew he had to use one more technique to make sure Jason wouldn't get up and come at him again. Jason's solar plexus, the nerve center of his entire body, was open and exposed, giving Lee the perfect opportunity to knock him out.

"Go for it, Lee!" Jeremy shouted.

It was now or never. Lee moved in for the final blow.

Chapter Eleven

As Lee raised his leg high to deliver a powerful naihanchi stomp to Jason's solar plexus, he heard someone shout "Stop!"

Lee's foot paused in midair as Suzanne Whittaker came running across the football field, her curly brown hair flapping around her face.

"Stop!" she cried again. Gasping, out of breath, she staggered to a stop near Jason and Lee. "Please stop!" she begged. "Please don't hurt my brother."

Suzanne's eyes were brimming with tears. Lee couldn't help feeling sorry for her, and even a little sorry for Jason, who lay motionless on the ground, groaning.

"Shut up, Suzanne!" Kevin cried. "Jason doesn't need your help. What are you trying to do? Make him look like a sissy?"

"Please, Lee," Suzanne begged. "Don't do it."

"No. Go ahead," said a new voice. "Give him what he deserves."

Lee slowly lowered his leg and turned around to see who was talking. To his surprise, it was Jason's father! Mr. Whittaker strode heavily across the field toward them, a grim look on his face.

"What are you waiting for?" Mr. Whittaker asked Lee. "You've got him where you want him. Finish him off."

Was this some sort of trick, Lee wondered? Had the entire Whittaker family jumped in here just to confuse him? There couldn't be any other explanation. Why else would Jason's father want him to hurt Jason more than he already had?

Lee studied the Whittakers carefully, waiting for some sudden move. Maybe Jason was going to leap up and start fighting again, or maybe Kevin was going to jump on his back, trying to slow him down. But Jason lay where he was. His eyes were closed, now, and he looked like he was in pain. Kevin looked down at his brother like he was about to cry, Suzanne was sniffling, and Mr. Whittaker glared at Jason with disgust.

"You call *this* being a winner?" Mr. Whittaker yelled down at Jason. "Letting some little pipsqueak of a kid knock you around like that? I didn't raise my kids to be losers. Get up and fight, *wimp!*"

Jason's eyelids fluttered open and he mumbled something that Lee couldn't understand. His father just looked disgusted. "You loser!" he shouted.

Lee didn't understand at all. Even though he'd just been ready to leave Jason in an unconscious heap, it was horribly unfair that Jason's own father would yell at him when he was lying on the ground like that. And even though Lee had beaten him in the fight, Jason was hardly a loser. Hadn't he just won the game for Midvale, like he did every week? What was his father talking about?

"Jason's not a loser!" Kevin defended his brother. "He's a hero!"

"What would you know about winning?" Mr. Whittaker yelled cruelly at Kevin. "You've never won a fight in your life. What am I wasting my money sending you to karate for? You still don't know how to throw a punch."

Kevin's face crumpled, and Lee saw a tear trickle out of the corner of his eye.

Lee shot a look at Michael and Jeremy. They looked just as confused as he felt. The most amazing part was that Lee was even feeling sorry for Kevin! Why was their father being so mean to both of them?

Lee backed away from Jason. He had a feeling that their fight wasn't so important anymore, compared to what was going on with Jason's father.

"Don't think I don't know how this happened," Mr. Whittaker said to Kevin. "I know Jason was sticking up for you, just like always. And it's because you're too chicken to fight your own battles. Well, don't expect your big brother to be around forever. Life's tough, kid, and if you want to be a success, you have to be tougher than the next guy. You gotta hit first, before they hit you. You're another loser."

"That's pretty funny, coming from you."

The voice was coming from near the ground. Jason struggled to sit up, and he stared at his father. One cheek was covered with dirt, and a lock of curly hair straggled over his eyes.

"What did you say?" Mr. Whittaker demanded.

"I said, you've got some nerve telling anyone he's a loser," Jason said, his voice getting a little stronger. "*You're* the one who's been out of work for a year."

"That's not my fault!" Mr. Whittaker thundered. "My company laid off three hundred people. There was nothing I could do about it."

"You could have looked for another job," Jason said, "instead of goofing off while mom works two jobs."

Mr. Whittaker walked a few steps over to Jason and stood over him. "First of all," he said, trying to keep from raising his voice, "I am not goofing off. I spent six months looking for work. Every day I scoured the want ads. I called everyone I know. But there's nothing out there. Nothing! Companies are only firing right now. Nobody's hiring."

"How would you know?" Jason demanded, managing to sit up all the way. "You stopped looking six months ago. You just gave up. Like a loser, a quitter!"

"I'm going to look again," Mr. Whittaker said. "As soon as I finish up a couple projects around the house."

With Kevin's help, Jason rose shakily to his feet. Standing, he was only a few inches shorter than his father. "You'll *never* be finished with those projects," he said. "The house has been a mess for the past six months, and why? Because you're hiding behind these so-called projects. Because *you're* the one who's afraid to face the tough world out there. So instead of worrying about your own life, you're always getting on my back, trying to turn *me* into a winner so you can feel better about yourself. Well, I'll tell you right now. I'm sick of it!"

Mr. Whittaker looked so angry, Lee was afraid he might do something violent, like hit his son. Lee felt his own legs tense, ready to rush in and defend Jason.

Just a minute ago, he'd been trying to hurt Jason himself. Now he wanted to help him!

Jason's father's face softened, and he shoved his hands in the pockets of his jeans. "Am I really doing that?" he asked softly.

Jason slowly nodded. Kevin and Suzanne moved closer to Jason, and Kevin put his arm around his brother.

"I'm trying not to be a loser, Dad," Kevin said, "but it's hard with you always telling me I am."

"I know you think you're helping us," Suzanne added, "but it's not working. It's too much pressure."

Mr. Whittaker pursed his lips, like he was thinking hard. "I *was* trying to help," he said. "I just figured if I trained you now, you'd have an easier time later on, when you grow up."

"If this is what it's like," Jason said, "then I don't think I want to grow up."

Mr. Whittaker looked more upset by that than anything Jason had said before. He put his arms around his son. "I'm sorry, Jason," he said. Then he wrapped his arms around his other two children, so that the four of them stood in a huddle. "I'm sorry for everything," he said. "I promise I'll think about what you said, okay?"

126

After a few seconds, Mr. Whittaker stepped back. "Who wants a ride home?" he asked.

"I do!" Kevin shouted.

"I'll walk," Suzanne said. "I want to talk to Michael for a minute."

"I'm gonna stick around too," Jason said. "I might throw a few practice shots. Just to let off some steam. You know."

Mr. Whittaker looked a little disappointed, but he nodded. "Come on, Kevin," he said.

As the two of them walked away, Jason turned and headed across the field, heading for the wooden scaffold with the hanging tire that stood at the side. Suzanne, the only one left, hesitantly approached Lee and his brothers.

"Hi, you guys," she said, sounding embarrassed. "I'm sorry you had to hear all that. I guess our dirty secret's out."

Michael patted Suzanne's arm. "There's nothing to be ashamed of," he said. "I'm sorry your father lost his job."

Ordinarily, Lee knew, Jeremy would have made fun of Michael for touching a girl. But now he was too busy reaching into his pocket, searching for a tissue to give Suzanne. He knew it was in there somewhere. He felt past his pencil stubs and rubber bands and his yo-yo and found it crushed at the bottom, crumpled, but relatively clean.

"Here," Jeremy offered.

Suzanne took the tissue and blew her nose. "Thanks."

"I'm sorry I called you a spy," Jeremy said, making a rut in the dirt with the toe of his sneaker. "I guess I didn't know what I was talking about."

"It's not the first time," Michael joked. "Well, I guess we should get home, too."

"Uh . . . can you guys wait a couple of minutes?" Lee asked, glancing over at the side of the field where Jason was shooting footballs through the hole in the tire. "There's something I've got to do."

"We'll be here," Michael promised.

Lee took off at a half-run down the field, heading straight for Jason. He slowed to a trot as he neared Jason. There were so many thoughts jumbled up inside his mind that he wasn't quite sure what he wanted to say. He just had to hope that he'd find the right words, and that Jason would listen.

Lee waited until after Jason had shot the last ball. Then Lee called out to him. "Hey!"

Jason started walking across the field with the

empty basket, ignoring Lee.

"Jason!" Lee said, running to keep pace with Jason. "I want to talk to you."

"I've got nothing to say," Jason said, stooping to pick up the first football. He threw it in the basket.

"I do," Lee said. "And I'm not leaving until you hear what I have to say."

"I heard everything you had to say this afternoon," Jason said. "Isn't it enough you won the fight? Or did you just want to rub it in?"

"I don't care about the fight," Lee said. "I *never* cared."

"So what do you want?" Jason asked. "And make it quick."

"I just wanted to say I'm sorry your dad doesn't have a job. I guess it's been rough on all of you."

Jason started walking toward the next ball in the grass, but he didn't walk quite so fast.

"I think I understand why you wanted to fight me," Lee said to Jason. "You were defending your brother. But there was no reason to, because I didn't do anything wrong by beating Kevin in kumite, and no one thought less of Kevin for losing. He's just a white belt. I'm a brown belt. He wasn't *supposed* to win. You overreacted to the whole situation."

Jason glanced at Lee for a second, then looked down. His sullen expression hadn't changed, but at least he was listening.

"And you're not proving anything by being a bully, either," Lee added. "You say you don't want to be like your father, but that's exactly what *he* does."

Jason's head jerked up abruptly and his eyes looked wounded. "I'm *nothing* like him," he insisted.

"I'm talking about the fact that you picked on me for the same reason your dad picks on you. 'Cause you were angry about something else," Lee said.

"Don't tempt me, Jenkins," Jason warned. "Just because you beat me once doesn't mean you can do it again. The way I act is none of your business."

"It is when it affects me," Lee said. "I just think you should build on all the good things you have, instead of making things worse. You're such a great athlete. You're the team hero. But you're angry a lot of the time. Sometimes you act like a bully. Our sensei at the karate school has a quote up on his bulletin board that says: 'He who conquers himself is the greatest warrior.' "

Jason laughed scornfully. "Oh, give me a break! Learning how to do karate chops is one thing, but don't give me any of that philosophy stuff. You sound like that guy on *Kung Fu*. Ah so, little grasshopper," he said, in a fake-sounding accent.

"Don't laugh," Lee said. "I know the quotes sound old-fashioned, but they're *true*. And they've helped me get through a lot of difficult situations."

"You don't know what difficult is in your big house with your rich parents. I know all about your famous mother. I saw her on a talk show talking about that stupid comic book robot she invented. Technotronic, or something."

"Turbotron," Lee said.

"Whatever," Jason said. "The point is, you don't know what difficult means. Difficult is having a father who's hiding behind his buzz saw and living in a house that looks like a construction site and never seeing your mother 'cause she works two jobs. But you wouldn't understand what I'm talking about."

For the first time since he'd spoken to Jason, Lee got angry. "Look at me!" he snapped. "Take a look."

Jason looked Lee up and down. "So?"

"So," Lee said, "it's obvious from my eyes and skin that I wasn't born into my family. I was born in Vietnam, and I still remember what it was like. I was born in a one-room hut made out of tin and cardboard. That's where I lived the first five years of my life with my grandfather and a family of rats. My mother died when I was born, and I never knew my father. There was never enough to eat. After my grandfather died, I had to live in a crowded orphanage with hundreds of other kids that nobody wanted. If my parents—my American parents, I mean—hadn't adopted me, I'd still be there. You think the way you live is bad, you should see where I used to live in Vietnam."

"I never thought about that . . ." Jason said slowly. "I mean, I knew you weren't born here, but I didn't really think about where you were from."

"It wasn't too easy when I got here, either," Lee said. "I was six years old, and I didn't speak any English, so they put me in kindergarten instead of first grade. Even now, people think I was left back." Lee was usually pretty quiet. He never talked about stuff like this—with anybody. But suddenly now it seemed that once he'd started talking, he couldn't stop. "But that was nothing compared to trying to get used to a whole new family and a new country and new customs. Everything was different. The food, even the way people eat is different here. I missed my grandfather. I missed seeing people who looked like me, who spoke my language. It was really hard. But I'm not telling you this because I want you to

132

feel sorry for me. That's my whole point. You have a choice how you react to things. You can either make the best of it, or you can make the rest of the world suffer just because *you* suffer."

Jason didn't say anything, but he didn't look angry either. He just looked thoughtful.

"Well, that's all I wanted to say," Lee said. He turned to leave.

"Lee . . ." Jason called after him.

Lee stopped.

"That karate stuff really works, huh?" Jason asked. "I mean, you can really take somebody out with those moves."

Lee sighed. Hadn't Jason understood a word he'd said? Was Jason going to join the dojo now, so he could have even more weapons to use against other people? "That's not the point," Lee said, disappointed.

"No, I know that," Jason said. "I just meant to say . . . you were right. I knew Kevin was faking about his limp. And I guess I suspected the truth about the bicycle tire. But I didn't care. I needed to punch somebody, and you were convenient."

Lee smiled. They were finally getting somewhere.

"But maybe you *weren't* so convenient after all,"

Jason said. "You're a pretty good fighter. I guess you showed me."

"I didn't want to," Lee said.

"I know," Jason said. "Shake?" He held out his hand and Lee shook it. The feud was over at last.

Lee smiled. Maybe he'd underestimated Jason after all. "I'll see you in school," he said.

"Yeah," Jason said. "See ya."

"You had the right idea all along, Michael," Lee said as he finished telling his brothers about his conversation with Jason. The three boys were walking their bicycles home, around the bend past the Bonny Brook Country Club.

"I should have done what you did and tried to 'understand' the enemy," Lee told Michael. "If I'd talked to Jason *before* the fight the way I did just now, maybe we never would have had the fight. Maybe we could even have been friends . . ."

Jeremy hooted. "With all the people in our school, you'd choose Jason Whittaker, even after everything that's happened?"

"I don't know," Lee said. "He didn't seem so bad when we were just talking . . ."

"I like that quote you told him," Michael said as they waited on a corner for the traffic light to turn green. " '*He who conquers himself is the greatest warrior.*' It really says a lot. I mean, in karate class we're supposed to pretend we're fighting this imaginary opponent who's the same size as us, but in a way, the opponent really *is* us. And the more we practice fighting 'ourselves,' the stronger we get."

"I know what you mean," Jeremy said, "but so far, my imaginary opponent is still winning over me. I don't think I'll *ever* learn to control myself."

"At least you're trying," Lee said.

"Which is more than Jason's done," Michael said. "And it's too bad, too. If he could beat himself, he'd be unstoppable, because right now he's his own worst enemy!"

"Oh, I don't know," Lee said. "I think he's gonna do okay." He smiled, thinking about all that had happened. First he'd been so worried about the fight. Then Jason had beat up Jeremy, and Lee's worst fears came true. Then Lee actually fought Jason, something he thought he'd never do. Finally, he'd gotten to know Jason a little better.

And he'd been surprised to find out he actually liked Jason. Now that all the bad stuff was over, he thought that maybe they could even learn to be friends someday.

"Don't be too hard on Jason, Michael," he said to

his older brother. "Especially you should give him a break. Now that you know what kind of pressure he's been under."

"I guess you're right," Michael said.

"I'm just glad the whole thing is over," Lee said. Jeremy raised his eyebrows.

"It is," Lee insisted. "Maybe Kevin won't become our best friend right away. Maybe he never will. But I don't have to feel afraid of his big brother anymore. And maybe when Kevin gets more advanced with his karate, he'll stop being his own worst enemy, too. Maybe Jason will be a good example for him."

"Maybe you're right," Jeremy said skeptically.

"I know I'm right," Lee said confidently.

The angry man will defeat himself in battle as well as in life.
                                        —Samurai saying

Glossary

Arigato—Thank you

Bo—(Weapon) Long wooden staff with tapered ends

Deshi—Karate student (below black belt level)

Dojo—Sacred hall of learning

Gi—Karate uniform

Hajime—Begin

Jyu-kumite—Freestyle sparring

Karate ni sente nashi—There is no first attack in karate

Karate—Empty-handed self-defense art

Kata—Form—an organized series of prearranged defensive and offensive movements symbolizing an imaginary fight between several opponents and performed in a geometrical pattern. Handed down and perfected by masters of a system of karate.

Kiai—Convergence of energy and spirit. Also refers to a loud shout used to startle or frighten an opponent.

KARATE CLUB

Kio-tsuke—Attention
Nunchuku—(Weapon) A flail. A pair of wooden
sticks attached by a cord.
Onegai-shimasu—Please teach us
Rei—Bow
Sai—(Weapon) A pair of iron sticks with U-shaped
handles, used to defend against sword attacks.
Seiza—Sit, kneeling
Sensei—Teacher or master
Shugo—Line up
Tai Chi Chuan—Chinese form of self-defense
Yame—Stop
Yoi—Ready

COUNTING

Ichi—One
Ni—Two
San—Three
Shi—Four
Go—Five
Roku—Six
Shichi—Seven
Hachi—Eight
Ku—Nine
Ju—Ten